Gigantic Failures

Disconnected Stories

Mark Anthony Cronin

Small Victories Press
Cleveland

First Small Victories Press Edition, June 2013

Gigantic Failures: disconnected stories:
stories by Mark Anthony Cronin
1st Small Victories Press Ed.

ISBN: 978-0-9891783-0-3

Cover and drawings by Robert Rhoads
Page design by Adam Robinson

Set in Caslon and Perpetua

For Nina and GG, who both used to tell me they wished I'd do something with my writing. At the moment this is the best I have to offer.

INTRODUCTION

Mark was one of the first new friends I made after graduating from college. This might not seem all that significant but it really is. High School sucks, right? College, if you go, can be great; you get to start over, reinvent yourself, and make new friends. The thing that you seem to forget during those four or five years is that the "real world" doesn't give a shit about you or your ideals or what you want to do with your life.

Soon after I graduated I moved back into my parent's basement and began working for a temp agency. This sucked. After a few months of third shift factory life where the closest thing I had to a conversation about the phases of feminism was siding with the guy who asked a co-worker to stop referring to the drive-thru girl at the McDonald's as the 'window bitch'—they settled on broad—I did gain some perspective.

Shortly thereafter I applied for and got a job at the bookstore I always shopped. My body and brain were still adjusting to being awake during the day and I had to interact with people constantly at the register, so it was a little rough in the beginning. Retail is a different kind of soul-diminishing work than manual labor but, rest assured, it can wear you thin. Some people can adopt or put on that personable-personality that they encourage you to have, Mark Cronin was hired a few weeks after I'd started and had some difficulties with this.

Babbling at the register trying to give Mark the rundown of keystrokes and item codes, I noticed that he wasn't giving me much in the way of hey-I'm-the-new-guy-at-work-and-really-want-to-seem-nice-and-hard-working-and-thanks-for-showing-me-the-ropes-stuff that is kind of standard when you are just starting out at a new job. I didn't really get it at first. Mark and I worked opposite schedules, being that we were the two newest team-members and both of us were being trained. Eventually though, our shifts started overlapping.

Mark had been given the Fiction section to run and he'd wheel his cart full of genre fiction authors passed me at the register, staring down with drooping eyes and a thin, tight mouth. I'd say something like 'hey man," with a friendly inflection, hoping for something more than his typical response of, 'hey,' short and mumbled.

Finally I decided to give up on that approach and asked him: 'Hey Mark. What's your deal? Are you always as upset as you look? Because it looks like you hate your life.' He glanced up and laughed a little wild laugh and flashed me a smirk. I knew there was a persona and it could be cracked.

I had a habit of carrying a pocket notebook around with me, which Mark noticed even though I rarely pulled it out to write at work—unfortunately there is a lot of work to be done in a used bookstore and there isn't a whole lot of time to sit around reading, none actually— and he asked me if I wrote. My answer to anyone who'd asked this question was that I used to write more but had since used the notebook for ideas I didn't want to forget. Mark nodded as I turned the question back on him.

After four months or so of asking Mark if I could read his stuff he brought in two stacks of paper and handed one to me and the other to a co-worker of ours. I knew after reading his stories, many of which are included here in *Gigantic Failures*, that Mark needed some kind of break because he was a much better writer than I imagined and that he would give himself credit for. After hearing that he got another rejection email and that he was done with writing I was inspired, inspired to write and share with him. This obviously was not an easy process for him. Writing and pouring over pages and pages of handwritten text, then heading to the library and typing for hours and hours until the public-use computer refused to let him log-in, Mark needed validation, he needed a writing buddy; anything that wasn't a dead end.

I started sharing ideas I had for stories with Mark and letting him in on some of my struggles and my lack of discipline. Essentially we commiserated for a while, consuming art films, doughnuts, beer, and books (most of the time separately.) Until one day I received a postcard from Mark. The text on the back began, 'Greetings from the Other Side....' and at the bottom was the Small Victories Press logo that is now on the spine of this book.

With a launching pad in place we put together two 'zines worth of material in a matter of months, got a printer, and started working.

We want everyone to feel worthwhile, get creative, find happiness, and do something they thought they would never be able to do. Get excited. The world will crush you if you can't find the right perspective.

It starts at the bottom. You are small and the mountain is impossibly big, with the summit far above you. You can see it, but who could jump that high? We don't really know where we are heading, but why not try up.

John B. Henry
March 2013

Gigantic Failures

"After I go out this door, I may only exist in the minds of all my acquaintances," he said. "I may be an orange peel."

—Teddy McAdle, *Nine Stories*

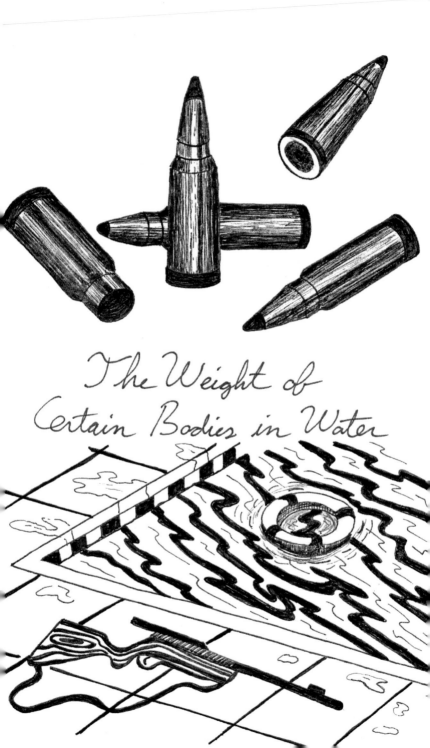

The Weight of
Certain Bodies in Water

They chipped the tiles at the bottom of the deep end, bullets rippling through the water of the pool the Boy swam in, tiny silver dots echoing through the blue. Sometimes they would embed themselves in the rough mortar, other times they'd ricochet and in slow motion force themselves up through the water, ebbing with tiny ringlets, out into the air, to disappear, like balloons made of lead, hovering up, further and further toward the atmosphere, until they were gone, out of sight.

There was the wavy orange and green silhouette of his father, a tower looming over the Boy, stretching his shadow out over the entire face of the pool, his scream muffled only by the water, becoming clear when the Boy came up to catch a breath, wincing in the sunlight splayed over the chlorinated surface.

"Come on, boy. Push yourself!"

Sometimes the Boy would hear the shell casings pinging off the concrete, or else he'd hear the cock, or a whoosh, as his father raised an arm, hand held onto the stock of the rifle, raising it up slowly with a fresh shot loaded into the chamber.

Only once did the Boy stay up long enough to hear the gun fire. It wasn't a pulse but a crack, like a whip. Birds would flap violently untangling themselves from the nearby trees and telephone wires, fluttering in a black spacious choreography before disintegrating into the clouds like specks of pepper into soupy mashed potatoes.

"We want you to be the best that you can be," the Boy's Mother told him one evening over dinner. "Being the best takes hard work, it takes dedication. Sometimes it even takes pain, great suffering. There are times when it's necessary for a person to die before his or her full worth reveals itself to the world."

After shoveling a forkful of green beans into her mouth she added, "To be the best you can't just train like the rest. You've got to go above and beyond. You have to be disciplined. You have to do things the other boys and girls wouldn't ever thing to try. Do you see that?"

The Boy nodded.

In school he didn't have any friends. He didn't make small talk or share laughs with the other kids. When he was around the whole atmosphere seemed to change and he learned quickly to just keep his distance.

The only place he felt safe was in the water. His only means of communication became quick little juts of his head accompanied by a hollow stare. His parents were essentially none existent when it came to matters outside of the pool. His teachers treated him like an apparition. He did all of his work and they were happy when it was turned in on time, especially since the Boy never asked questions during class. He was a ghost. Even as he grew up and filled out and stubble started coming through on his cheeks and chin it was as if he'd been born transparent. No one seemed to see him as a person. No one cared unless he was in the water where they'd said he painted portraits of angels in the waves.

It was the Boy's Mother who'd had the idea of shaving him from head to toe and coating him in a thin layer of Vaseline which she applied herself. She felt it would make the Boy more 'aerodynamic,' and of course he didn't complain.

She'd sit on the lid of the toilet and use a disposable razor to shave him and when he was as bare as a baby she'd glob on the jelly, making his flesh burn and glisten.

"I want you to move like the water moves, become a part of it," she said one of the times the two of them were in the bathroom, "blend in, become invisible…"

The whole thing with the rifle came about the first time the Boy got into the pool. He had had no idea what he was doing, in fact, he did more struggling than he did actual swimming, and so to give the Boy some motivation his Father went and got the rifle, loaded it, and fired three shots into the deep end. The claps shook the Boy to his core, like thunder during a storm: one two three, bam bam bam…

He'd wept under the water, hoping maybe his Father would think his red eyes were a result of the chemicals in the pool.

The gunshots didn't cause him to bat an eyelash after a few months. The initial fear was intense and demanded a response, but since then the rifle had become like chamber music to the Boy, an instrument in the chorus of his song.

When he did finally start to compete the Boy won six junior championships, went on to nab four gold pennants for the gymnasium of his junior high school and six more for George Washington High.

On his own the Boy had beaten every state record there was to beat and had rows of trophies at home, on shelves, in his room, trophies which his mother took extra special care to clean once a week, adding the detail into her normal routine, taking up a special bucket and towel just for the Boy's room, for his trophies, which she'd marvel at, thinking about all the Boy had accomplished with the tools she'd given him to succeed.

In the Sedgwick Swim-o-thon, at Regionals, and Finals the Boy placed first. He'd been placed in the brackets of at least two major World Championships, and in his senior year of high school he'd become the most sought after swimmer in the United States. He could have gone anywhere, totally free. There were even talks of the 2000 Olympic Games to be held in Sydney, Australia, under the breaths of some very powerful individuals who'd been watching the Boy since he'd been at Bunyan Elementary.

The endorsement offers were coming in daily. Reps would call or just show up with duffel bags full of gear: goggles, Speedos, sweatshirts, flip flops, wet shoes; all types of things: sun tan lotions and topical gels and gaudy cardboard cut-outs with the face blanked out and in bold block letters it'd say: This Could Be You!

All of it was left at the front door or had begun piling up in the foyer.

The Boy's parents went on to do several interviews with local news stations, convincing themselves they were absorbing for the Boy all the difficulties of the spotlight and attention as questions of what the Boy would do in the future became the only thing anyone talked about in their hometown.

Then came the day the Boy's Father woke up and heard no splashes in the pool, heard no sounds at all besides his wife's snoring. The Boy had run away, though at that point he was closer to being the Man he would become.

He'd walked out of his family's home, never to return. He carried nothing with him besides a toothbrush he had tucked into the pocket of the flannel shirt he wore. No bags. No mementos. He hitchhiked or scrounged for bus fare, eventually making his way to Michigan where it was said he swam the entire hundred and eighteen mile width of the thumb that is that state's lake, emerging before a crowd of beachgoers stark naked before walking into a nearby patch of trees and disappearing.

Back home the Boy who'd gone missing became a phenomenon. Within days people knew the story and had inflated it with all the gossipy details one would expect from a small town enterprise.

In Michigan the Man was becoming a legend: who was he? What was he doing? Where had he gone?

Several eyewitnesses reported seeing him stripping on the opposite beachhead. Some fishermen said they'd towed him part of the way. Papers ran their own take on the event and people continued to talk, all of the stories conflicted and merged into one. No one had seen him clear enough to give an accurate description. The Man was an enigma. A local reporter dug up what she could and began a correspondence with a fellow back in Kansas who fed her all the background details through emails and faxes.

Four days later a cattle farmer passing through Cleveland on his way back to Iowa reported the he found the Man on the side of the highway, wrapped him in a down blanket he'd found in the cab of his truck (again the Man was naked), and drove him to an area hospital where he said the Man got out and ran behind some bushes and was gone.

It was as if he were a vapor leaving no trail, an afterthought of his real self, or else a dream, conjured up by all the people who were inadvertently tied to the story that was unfolding before their eyes.

Off the coast of Guatemala a kid who'd been searching for American quarters in the sand on a beach near Puerto San Jose told the local press that he recognized the Man from the cover of a magazine his father stocked at his shop.

According to the kid the Man had come out of the Pacific Ocean and when the kid asked him for an autograph the Man said nothing, walked into a restroom nearby, and never came back out. The kid, baffled, had gone in to check it out and found no trace of the Man.

Speculations grew more obscure and far reaching, becoming science fiction: He's not human, He's a ghost. His body is somehow able to evaporate and rematerialize at his will.

There were no reasonable explanations. Word spread from coast to coast, continent to continent. The Man's parents were found and interviewed by all major newscasters and radio jockeys and talk show personalities around the world.

On one of the early morning national gigs the Man's mother stared into the camera and proclaimed, "I tell you all here and now, my boy will disappear beneath the waves; my beautiful baby boy will finally be reborn in the womb of the sea."

The Man's Father said nothing, sitting dejectedly on the couch while an uncomfortable hush fell over the audience and hosts. His face had begun to droop from the weight of his age and his hair had whitened. Something deep behind his eyes was speaking, louder than any image projected, and it was that of loss, grief, and torment. The Mother was considered totally insane, putting herself on display as some type of mystic, draped in jewelry and silk scarves and heavy cloth hanging in loose bundles from her body, seemingly basking in the all the coverage he son's story was getting.

It didn't take long for the holes to get filled in, whether it was with factual details or embellished yarns. The ammunition was obtained and all conclusions were unanimous: the parents were loons, detached from the world, in dire need of bathing and deep psychological help. All necessary frills were added and manipulations were made from production to production. The Man as a boy had been ruthlessly tortured and beaten into nothingness, a void. None of the basic human emotions that were inherent in all were within him and he was purging himself of even his body, whether metaphorically or literally. Maybe he was already dead, a ghost, or a hush on the wind, the white cap of a wave breaking in the tide. Maybe he didn't even exist anymore but had become a branding on the conscience of the entire world, a symbol of abuse and withdrawal. The Boy was trying to set the Man free and the Man was trying to do the same for the Boy.

Sightings continued to come in droves: a young woman had given the Man shelter in Los Angeles, where it was said he'd been swimming canals from California to Mexico. Footage from a security camera showed the Man (or what people took to be him) swimming in a public pool in Truth of Consequence, New Mexico. A maid found him in the kiddy pool of her employer's yard in Miami, and when she approached him he startled awake and hopped a privacy fence.

It was said there was a tape of him swimming the English Channel.

A couple saw him poke his head up out of the water of the Tunnel of Love.

It all became too much, a bloated exaggeration.

He'd been given plenty of nicknames. In select circles the Man's stature grew biblical. He was seen as some kind of god. The oral traditions of thousands of years ago told of him in the esoteric ways all prophecies speak to their believers, in labyrinths and coded messages.

Still it was thought amongst these people that the Man was sent as a sign of an end, or a new beginning, or of *something* to come. The Man's name was erased, totally forgotten. He became something beyond himself: a sermon given unto the world, connecting the followers of his acts through telephone wires and published reports.

The first sustained glimpse of the Man came in Cape Cod, in a small diner set outside a little sea breeze town.

By then the entire world was familiar with him: they'd seen the photographs his parents had submitted to the media and even the composites done by a sketch artist working for the FBI, who'd compounded the two years the Boy had been gone and showed what he would look like as the Man, with a fully grown beard and fitter from swimming so much. They said his skin would be dark and tough looking like jerky, all the time in the sun, all the exposure to the elements. As he stood before the customers and workers at the diner however, living and breathing, they found he looked nothing like the pictures. He was pale and rigid, his skin nearly translucent, the tissue of his lips flaked off like fish food, and his eyes were shallow, pupils dilated to fixed points, dark as well water. His arms hung off his body like wet spaghetti, fingers pruned, shrunken and skinny and utterly old looking.

The only part of his body that was sustained was his legs, which looked healthy and muscular.

He wore a pair of running shorts that didn't fit well and a faded gray t-shirt pocked with holes and covered in stains. If they hadn't known him from the television they would have mistaken him for a bum.

Despite his ragged appearance some of the old timers present at the diner said the Man had an aura about him, that it seemed as if he glowed a little bit, in a kind of heavenly light; and that it was possible even that he was haloed, like one of the early saints whose portraits were cast in oils and housed in those old weathered frames and musty glass hanging on the walls of museums or in the halls of cathedrals.

He'd come in and stood at the counter. Intuitively a waitress got his a glass of water. She'd say later that she 'felt' him speaking to her on some deeper level than words could communicate. They'd all, the customers and workers alike, tell reporters that just as quickly as he'd entered the diner he exited, without a word spoken or a glance given to anyone in the room.

It'd been two years since the Boy had run away. Two years since the first sightings of the Man on the shores of Lake Michigan. Two years. And still there were people affected by it more than just reading the occasional headline or seeing the national update.

The Boy's Father had taken all of his grief and guilt and shoved it way down into the pit of his stomach until it ate through him thoroughly enough for him to do the only thing he could think to do: go to the pool with the rifle.

Just before committing what to some looked like just a random, if not strange, act, the Boy's Father aimed the rifle at the deep end, as he had done all those times with his son swimming, but instead of firing he tried to draw the discarded shots back into the chamber, draw out all the rounds he'd carelessly fired into the pool. What he wished to do was draw back time, to that first day he'd brought out the rifle, he'd pull his son out of the water, hold him close, whisper to him that he loved him and that it hurt him to see his Boy not able to do something, to see him struggling. That was all. But there was no going back, and realizing this the Boy's Father did the only thing he could to stop the pain: fired a final round from the rifle.

Three days after appearing in the diner an anonymous tip came in that the Man had been seen sitting on a bench near the town square and hadn't moved in quite some time.

Every reporter and news anchor was sent out. A convoy of white vans with different logos painted on their sides rolled up with screeches and surrounded the area where the Man had been seen. There was definitely someone on the bench, but it was impossible to make out whether it was actually him or not. Whoever it was didn't flinch as the crews rolled out their gear and set up, drawing long cords from the van's terminals to the cameras. Microphones and other various electronic devices were checked and re-checked. There was no way they were going to let this slip from their fingers. Women anchors powdered their faces and the men checked their hair in the side mirrors of their stations respective van. Some of the cameramen smoked cigarettes listlessly, still hoisting the large boxy cameras on their shoulders. A few of the town's deputies cordoned off the entrances and exits into the square to ensure a riot didn't occur when the news broke. Already people from nearby homes, various shops, and restaurants started to converge on the scene and talk. No one was missing a beat.

Back up was called.

Cameras, lights, open notepads, and foam topped microphones were all set and ready, lumped like a massive tumor on the square. Everyone was on: a blob of flesh, polyester, and muddled voices circled now by a larger growing ring of faces, all behooved and mystified and curious.

Cigarettes were extinguished and lenses were focused. Someone was already asking if the Man was dead. Things were being written and shots were being gauged.

"It's a historical moment here in Cape Cod as we finally—" a collective voice chimed.

From where he sat he could see through a divide in some trees the water of the Atlantic Ocean, as clear as a sheet of paper laid out on a table top.

The mob had condensed into a swarm buzzing with all the tormented sounds bees make when they become agitated. The Man knew they were there, teeming at his back with that same liquid like quality to their movements as water had just before it rushed over him; the cold palm of the Atlantic: a mirror reflecting only itself against the sky; and there he was, hovering above it, as the people and sounds receded into darkness, his eyes closed, a second passing into nothing, no more time. Simply the sea reflecting sky and vice versa.

There were days when the Boy would go out to the pool in his parent's backyard. He'd lower himself into the cold water. He didn't swim laps of practice his backstroke, instead he'd let the air escape his lungs and he'd sink to the bottom, where he could sit for a while, weightless and absent from the world.

A Portrait of the Actor
as the Actor as Himself

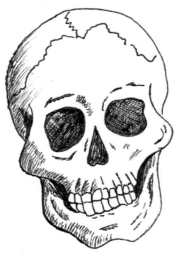

The Actor has just completed a very tough scene in which the character he is playing has learned that his wife has died in a terrible accident and it is upon him, the character the Actor is playing, to go to the hospital and positively identify the body. The character is absolutely falling to pieces in the scene, and so it was upon the Actor to fall to pieces as well. A character is only as believable as the Actor allows him to be and this particular scene was very tough on the Actor, not just in terms of the Actor being forced into a place where emotion must be conveyed by a character he is playing, but also in the sense of finding that emotion inside himself, and where exactly it comes from.

The Actor is sitting in his dressing room, staring at himself in the dressing room's mirror, wondering how he's kept up the act for so long and when it'll end. He's never had a wife, nor has he been called to a hospital morgue to identify the body of someone he loved, but he is a human being: a complex individual with fears and frustrations and hardships and sadness. Death is still a reality the Actor knows he will face one day. And so he's decided, after he's returned to the set and done the next scene, (which is really when the character the Actor is playing loses it, banging his fists into the floor and weeping.) if the Director asks him "Where do you find this kind of raw emotion?" Which the Actor knows from experience directors are sometimes known to do, the Actor, in response, will say simply that it all comes from within, as in from *inside* the Actor, which is something the Actor feels the Director will be able to walk away with feeling ok about having placed the responsibility of such a complex and multi-layered character in the hands of such a talented and empathetic actor.

Objéct Permanence

This was a little bit after we'd broken up, but she'd come over with the kid and I'd hear her honk the horn and go out there in mesh basketball shorts and a ratty old t-shirt with my shoe's heels tucked uncomfortably under my feet and I'd duck down next to her car and pop up next to the window making some sort of silly noise the kid loved to hear and the kid would just laugh and laugh and I'd laugh and laugh and I'd just keep doing that, over and over, and we'd all be laughing so hard sometimes I'd tear up, not like crying or nothing, but you know how you get when you're laughing so hard. You just can't help it.

Sometimes too I'd glance in the side mirror and the girl would be looking back at me doing my bit and she'd be smiling like the kind of smile you give someone you like or whatever, real flirtatious I guess. Sometimes I'd smile back, but mostly I just played with the kid. The kid's laugh was like a drug to me. I'd take in all I could then she'd pull away and I'd go back inside, drink two Schlitz's, and fall asleep for nine hours until I had to be at work. I was working at a gas station. It technically wasn't third shift but it was basically third shift and I fucking hated the job, hated the fact that I'd dumped all of my savings into the girl and her kid, not so much the kid but definitely the girl, only to be left with these brief moments of hearing the kid laugh then watching him go away. That's basically saying I was left with nothing, and that shit hurts, for real. Especially after what I went through: being there for all of it: the pregnancy, the birth, the hospital stay. I didn't sleep for four days because I wanted to be sure the kid was ok, because it was jaundice and had to be kept in one of those incubator things and then wrapped in some special blanket that made it look like a glowworm. Doesn't that deserve *something*? I mean damn man, what the fuck?

But whatever, that's life, right?

I'd take money through a slot and hand change back through a slot or I'd pass cigarettes through a slot. The owner of the gas station felt it'd been robbed to many times so he had these thick ass panes of like polymer plastic or some shit put up so there's the slot and a speaker and ain't no way anyone's getting back there, not even with like a bomb or something. The shits that thick.

Sometimes I think the glass is like a metaphor or whatever it is that you call it when you say one thing but mean another, but I can't decide what the metaphor is or what I'm even really talking about really. I get that way sometimes. I can't help it.

I remember this one time when I was still with the girl and the kid and she was telling me how the kid learned to like perceive reality and shit. I just didn't get it. She'd read all the books like the what to expect and all that so she was really smart when it came to the kid, only this one time she told me that it was hard for her to love it because whenever she looked at him, the kid, she saw her ex, or as she referred to him 'the sperm donor,' which I always thought was really fucked up but I didn't ever say shit because I wanted to be with her and loved her and the kid. But so this one time she's explaining this shit called like object permanence and how like the kid doesn't know that things are always there or whatever... like I said I didn't really understand it all, but so what I do know is like when I bend down and pop up and the kid laughs he's laughing because he thinks I disappeared and then I'm back all of a sudden. So it got me sad afterward, after me and the girl had broken up and shit, because it's like the kid won't even know I existed. He's got no idea I was even really there or if he did it's just like *poof*, I'm gone and not coming back. Oh well.

Now tell me that's not the saddest fucking thing you've ever heard?

The girl came by one day with the kid but the kid was asleep so I didn't get to do my bit and the girl said she wasn't coming back around anymore because she'd met some guy on Facebook or MySpace or some shit who was over in Afghanistan and when he got back they were getting married.

This is what she tells me the last day I ever see her and the kid and the kid was asleep so I didn't get to do my bit and get the drug I needed to sleep. I got real emotional and almost kicked the side of her car. I wanted to so fucking bad, but I didn't. I started crying (yeah yeah) and then she pulled away and I hurried up and ran inside the trailer and got my keys and followed her to where she was going, which ended up being a grocery store up the street.

Don't be thinking I was going to do anything crazy like steal the kid or some shit because I wasn't. I just watched her walk around the aisles with the kid still in the car seat in the cart she was pushing. She never noticed me. She was on her cell phone most of the time probably texting her new boyfriend over in Afghanistan, if that's even possible. I don't know. But I felt like a ghost or something, just haunting them or some shit, so I left. I drove home that day with a huge weight on my chest. It felt how it did the day Ricky Morcho hit me in the chest with a baseball bat when we were twelve and I wouldn't let him on my team in homerun derby because my dad told me never to trust spicks and especially never let them on your team because they are backstabbers. So I told him that, Ricky, I said, "you can't be on my team you backstabbing spick," and he hit me with a Louisville Slugger right in the sternum and I broke his nose and after that dad took me to Urgent Care and when we were driving home he gave me my first beer because he always had a cooler in the truck with him. So that's how it felt. Not like drinking the beer and feeling good because I broke Ricky's nose but really fucking painful because when he hit me it really fucking hurt, so like that, like the pain part.

The kid wouldn't remember me and the girl would never tell him who I was or what I had been to him at one point or anything. I'm sure she's cut all my pictures out of the scrapbooks we made for the kid, and thrown away or sold all the books I bought the kid and wrote notes in for the kid to read one day about how much I love the kid and his mom and all that, which is still true, in terms of the kid. I really do love that fucking kid, but what do I have now? The ghosted feeling and the glass and the understanding of what object permanence is, and now that I'm thinking about it I think I remember what the metaphor is that I was trying to think of earlier.

Daedalus, the Bastard!

The neighbor's god damn kid shot the swimming pool with his BB gun, Rodney Cafner notices as he's taking out the trash. He is out there now with some special water proof duct tape he bought for some other projects months before, trying to seal the hole at least from the outside where the pool is now bulging out at the bottom and spraying a single steady stream through a sewing needle sized hole. It's a cheap pool: the kind that's plastic and has no real support to it other than the water. Rodney, his wife, and Kal, their son, had to stand around the thing and lift the sides as the water rose up from the bottom, coming out of the head of a garden hose attached to the spigot on the back of the house. This was on the day he'd brought it home nearly ten years ago. He'd bought it at Wal-Mart and it was cheap but had stood the test of time, and it was his, Rodney's, and he's out there now on his hands and knees trying to repair the god damn thing, tearing off strips of the special water proof duct tape with his teeth, mumbling obscenities to himself all because Rodney has seen the kid with the BB gun, and what the hell is a kid that age doing with a BB gun anyway? Rodney thinks. He can't be older than nine or ten.

The father, David or Daniel Sally, the hotshot, probably doesn't even care what his kid is doing anyway. The kid is a nuisance all over the neighborhood, always shooting at passing cars or pets or houses across the way. Now, Rodney's pool.

Something needs to be done about that boy, Timmy or Tommy or maybe Thomas is his name. Either way something needs to be done. Kal would have never done anything like this. The best kind of son a father could ask for: never got in trouble; never went around and caused a ruckus or hurt anyone, such a good kid; never talked back; never really even needed to be punished or talked to seriously. He was always respectful and got good grades in school and had a lot of friends. At his graduation from Roosevelt High School he had no trouble kissing and hugging his family, shaking his father's hand for a photograph. He smiled and was happy to make everyone proud. Had a cumulative GPA of 4.1, which Rodney didn't even know was possible. Got into Cornell because of it.

It's easy to imagine the Sally boy as the antagonist of several major conflicts with other children and teachers before getting expelled; the Sally's being forced to move from city to city to enroll him into new high schools until finally he gives up and drops out, and if his parents are smart, which Rodney tends to think they're probably not, will kick him out of their house whereby he'll be disposed to a life of petty crime and heavy drug use and either incarceration or overdose or some worse fate at the hands of a drug fiend or some petty lowlife criminal, any of which sounds harsh but then again these are the ways thing catch up with people and it's impossible to tell them otherwise.

Kal lives and works in New York City, at a major publishing house Rodney can never remember the name of but knows it's big and publishes a lot of the newest and best-selling books by people's favorite authors. Kal himself is working on a novel and when he and Rodney talk on the phone Kal enumerates at length about concepts Rodney has no idea about. He's so smart. Rodney doesn't know where he gets it. Maybe Doria, Rodney's wife, Kal's mother. She was so smart, so beautiful, and had so much. She'd be proud of Kal, Rodney knows.

There is no medical explanation for her condition. Doctor after doctor has been baffled by it. One day the lights just went out and she's been catatonic; totally unresponsive. For almost ten years now Rodney has had to listen to doctors and specialists say they're sorry in a myriad of ways. Nothing changes. Rodney would have taken an explanation even if it was followed by "incurable" or "very rare" anything to give it a name, a form that could be pondered and rationalized and brought to terms. But no, all he has are apologizes and the feeling of faint hope that at any moment she could simply snap out of it and come back to him, at the same time knowing this will never happen.

Rodney stands with an *oomph* and a clutching, then a sigh and a limp. He's not getting any younger. His trousers are damp.

"Damn it," he says out loud to himself, brushing at the flecks of dirt and grass stuck to the spots on this knees. He'd only come out to take the trash to the can. Now he's going to have to go over to the Sally's place and talk to the father.

Inside Doria is right where he left her, sitting a bit slumped in her wheelchair with her gaze fixed absently on the television screen. It is a rerun of *Days of Our Lives*, a show she had once loved.

"I have to run next door, dear," Rodney says, leaning in to kiss Doria on the forehead, "I'll be right back."

Rodney knows she's not going to say anything or even register what he's saying to her but he has to do it or he feels he'll come undone. This feeling had come over him a few times: this kind of unraveling, as if the very cells that made up his body were coming apart.

It'd started with the one young punk specialist who Rodney had taken Doria to see. This punk had sat high and mighty in his chair and offered nothing all the other doctors and specialists hadn't already offered, only this punk added, "This is a very odd case, maybe could be worth some serious grant money. Your wife would make a great case study."

It took every fiber of Rodney's being not to beat the life out of him right there in the office. And since then Rodney finds himself occasionally willing himself to exist, whether it be during his bathing of Doria or as he reads to her at night from the broken spine paperbacks she used to carry around in her purse all of the time or in the yard, at the store. It can happen anywhere.

Rodney refuses to accept help, tells everyone he has it handled, using his will and his love to carry on despite all of the mess and heartache. He'd decided early on he'd have to do things on his own. Doria is his wife and that's the way it will be, even if she's locked in the house inside of her head watching the syndicated episodes of soap operas through a pair of binoculars.

It had been Kal who found his mother. She'd asked him to go to the store and buy a gallon of milk. She had been making macaroni and cheese.

After some half-hearted protest he walked the few blocks to the drug store and bought the milk. All in all he was probably gone for fifteen or twenty minutes. When he got home he found his mother standing at the stove, vacantly staring out the small window over the sink, a pot of water boiling over onto the burner on the stove, hissing loudly.

"The labyrinth is the only feasible model of the Universe," he says now, sitting leaned off the edge of the couch in his apartment's living room with his friend Elijah seated next to him, totally slumped into the cushions of the couch with his feet on the table. Kal is working seeds out of a bud of marijuana so he can roll another joint. "I mean think about it," he goes on, rolling little bits of the bud between his index finger and thumb, "The progression in just the last fifty years is staggering: computer systems, Internet, GPS navigation systems, smart phones... We've mapped the fucking world and yet we're more lost than ever because the shits so complex and convoluted it's impossible to, you know, like...navigate. It's a maze."

Elijah grunts and snorts phlegm into his throat, swallows loudly, and says, "that-was-mind-*BLOW*-ing," then laughs, very high still from the first joint the two of them smoked just minutes ago.

"Shut the fuck up," Kal says, licking the rolling paper. "You're just mad because in that subhuman doped out mind of yours you're trying to understand what I'm even talking about. You retarded dick-less fuck."

"Whoa man, I don't believe I intended this to go so far as insult so just chill, alright?" Elijah says, half serious.

Kal only looks at him with a look of feigned contempt and lights the joint and takes a long drag then passes it back to Elijah and is immediately struck by a cascade of images all overlapping and expanding inside of his mind: rapid speed pull back of the Earth: he sees the divisions of agricultural territories and cities residential plans all mapped out and coming together, things growing and erecting themselves in instances faster than light, then: televisions, computer screens, telephones, cell phones, all connected through wires draped over the cities and towns and farms, all of it spanning on into a horizon that never ends, only bends; the sun never actually setting, the world staying in constant flux. He sees the world as it rotates in space. It begins spinning faster and faster until it is an orb and then blue haze: an endless number of cycles and systems all interchanging and aligned. He sees the Google map app directions to his parents' house in St. Louis: a blue line cut through a cartoon United States: turn right, turn left. Go 454 miles then exit right. He sees his parents waving from the lawn as he's pulled back into his head by the beam of light he's ridden through the scene. It's all happened in just a few seconds. He is still on this couch and Elijah is trying to pass back the joint but Kal declines. "You go ahead," he says.

"No way am I finishing this thing by myself. I have got to take a ten pound shit."

Kal leans forward and opens the drawer on the under-side of the coffee table, from it takes an orange prescription bottle and stands, walking to the kitchen sink where he shakes two pills from the tube and pops them into his mouth, cups enough water in his hand, and swallows them down.

"What are those?" Elijah calls out from the couch.

"They're for anxiety," Kal says. "They wouldn't help you."

He is standing there in the kitchen staring at the off white space above the sink. The words barely feel like his own as they leave his mouth. He closes his eyes and pinches the bridge of his nose. In the background he hears Elijah shuffle off to the bathroom and he wonders what his father is doing right at that moment.

Inside the Cafner's home the phone is ringing. On the television screen a dam is crumbling and millions of tons of water are pouring through the rubble and debris into the empty river bed beyond. The scene then jumps to an all-white room where an actor playing a doctor steps out stage left, complete in white medical gown, and says, "Ever feel *this* way during a bowel movement? Use Pudamue, it's guaranteed to work."

Rodney, still in his graying white t-shirt and damp slacks, walks up his driveway to the sidewalk and crosses over to the Sally drive, up a walkway, to the house's foyer's entrance, where he presses the doorbell's button on the door frame, immediately stuffing his hands in his pockets to wait. Why do there need to be so many doors? Rodney thinks.

No one comes.

He waits a moment and rings the doorbell again. After a few seconds there is movement inside the house. The door that connects the foyer to the house whooshes, Rodney hears, then the foyer's main door opens just enough for the Sally boy's father to peak his head out at Rodney.

"Rod," the father says with surprise, "to what do we owe the pleasure?"

"Well, actually Dave," Rodney gambles, "we've got a bit of a situation here." And feels better when David doesn't correct him on the name, "You see—"

David holds up a finger, "I'm going to throw on some footwear, just give me two seconds alright buddy." He says, disappearing behind the doors, reappearing a moment later with shoes slipped on, the heels tucked under his feet, "ok Rod, what's up?"

"Have you got a minute to take a quick walk with me?"

"Sure thing," David says, welcoming Rodney to cut across the lawn to get back to his own driveway.

"As I'm sure you're aware your boy—"

"Timmy," David interjects casually.

"As I'm sure you know *Timmy* can be quite the nuisance, and I'm afraid this time, well..." Rodney invites David to look at the pool, which has since sprung its leak once more—the tape having lost its adherence and fallen off onto the ground—not only from the original tiny hole but now in a shower head like pattern of the original and a ring of much smaller holes, the side bulging absurdly, like an alcoholic's gut under a tight t-shirt.

"Oh my," David says, putting his open palm over his mouth and rubbing his clean shaven cheeks, "huh."

Inside Rodney can hear that the phone is ringing, "Could you excuse me for one second?" He says.

"Of course."

Rodney leaves David standing there and jogs into the house, picking up the receiver off its base, "Hello?"

"Dad, it's Kal," his son says at the other end of the line.

"Kal, hi... I'm a little busy right now, there's a bit of a situation here right now, his son shot the pool. Could I call you back in just a few minutes?"

"The pool?" Kal says.

"Yeah, can you believe it, things been out there for years and not a problem but it's probably ruined now."

Rodney sighs.

"Dad there is something I really need to talk to you about. Um, I just... I really need to talk to you, ok?"

"I'll call you back in just a couple of minutes. I just need to handle this. The neighbors over here now and he's... Well, let me call you back. Just a few minutes, ok?"

"Ok," Kal says, and hangs up.

Rodney sets the phone down and takes a quick peek in at Doria.

Back outside David's eyes are glued to the screen of a Blackberry.

"So," Rodney says, as David slips the phone back into his pocket, "how do we want to handle this Dave?"

"Well, I'm obviously happy and willing to reimburse you for the pool Rod, that's a given. Was there something else you were thinking?"

"Well I think I speak for the entire neighborhood when I say that boy of yours–"

"Timmy." David says.

"When I say Timmy maybe needs to get a talking to, or maybe some sort of punishment for his actions, he needs to learn he can't–"

"Trust me Rod, as your neighbor and as part of this community I hear ya loud and clear. No static whatsoever, and as Timmy's father I can assure you that me and my wife are doing everything within our power to raise an intelligent and obedient child but, well, Timmy... and I don't mean to bring this up as an excuse, but Timmy is having a hard time of it right now. He was recently diagnosed with ADHD and arising Schizophrenia. It's greatly affected all of us, especially him, obviously. He's on a couple different medications and they haven't exactly synched up yet. He's just not been himself lately. So for that I am sorry, both Carol and I are, really Rod, and as I already said I have absolutely no problem reimbursing you for the pool, none at all."

Rodney feels instantly ashamed and lets his head drop, "Shit David," he says, "I'm sorry... Jesus, if I'd have known, I wouldn't... you know my wife–"

David puts up a hand, "Really Rod, no problemo. My son caused damage to your property and I want to pay you back. Our own personal issues as a family don't change the circumstances here, so please, just tell me, how much would you like for the pool?"

* * *

Kal lay on his back, one hundred percent horizontal, in his bed, with his arms tucked up under his back and his legs pushed so tightly together his knees rub and it's painful.

Elijah's finished in the bathroom and the faint odor is wafting in under the door where he now stands outside Kal's room, knocking and saying, "Hey Kal, what's going on? I thought we were going to watch that movie or whatever."

Kal hasn't said a word. The room is spinning only it isn't. On his desk he can see the stacks of pages that comprise his book. He desperately wants to talk to his father, needs to talk to him, right now. Kal lays there in his bed and the room seems to spin only he knows it's in his head and so to steady himself he traces the intricate maze like stitching in the mattress under the sheet, waiting for the phone to ring, desperately, even torturously, with Elijah just outside, no longer knocking or talking but just standing there, with his ear pressed against the faux wood grain of the bedroom's thin door.

"Let's just say it'll never happen again and you'll talk to Timmy about it, when he's fully ready and acclimated to the dru– to the medications, and that'll be that." Rodney says, to David, who's already shaking his head and reaching into his back pocket.

"Nonsense," David says, and takes out his wallet, thumbing through some bills, "how about I give you fifty bucks just for the sake of conscience and reasonable neighborly etiquette?"

"Ok," Rodney says with a sigh.

The phone starts to ring again.

Not even a second passes between the ring and a loud rip like paper being torn and the rush of water as the pool splits down its pregnant side and dumps its contents on the grass and the driveway and even onto Rodney and David, who both scamper and leap in the air trying to dodge the wave as it rides itself out somewhere near the chain link fence that divides Rodney's from David's property and the back porch's third and highest step on Rodney's house, the pool imploding on itself, it's sides de-blooming, like a flower in reverse.

The phone is still ringing.

"My God," Rodney says with a cackle. He can't believe the thing held that much water.

"Jesus," David says, and then: "as we agreed," trying to pass the bills over to Rodney who's just to stunned to think about them there, hanging in David's hand, as David sops in his shoes and surveys the lawn and himself, his soaked shoes and pants; the splash on his shirt.

"I'm sorry," Rodney says and steps around David's still outstretched hand with the bills to squelch his way back into the house to yet again answer the phone, fumbling it up off the base just in time to say hello to a dead line.

There's a small address book Rodney keeps in the junk drawer under the kitchen counter. He sets down the receiver and rummages through the drawer trying to find the book. He sometimes takes it out to call an old friend or a relative out-of-state and sets it somewhere and forgets about it, "Damn it," He says out loud to himself. Why doesn't he just have Kal's number memorized by now? He shouldn't need the stupid book for his own son's phone number.

"...felt this way..." The television says in the other room.

Rodney gives up trying to find the book in the mess of rubber bands, hand tools, pens, envelopes, bouncy balls, scratched lottery tickets, curled discarded photographs, and slams the drawer shut totally mad at himself not only for having misplaced it again but for everything: getting David over here, when his son is...if he had known he never would have. He sighs.

Kal is still on his back, staring at the ceiling. The receiver of his bedroom's telephone is hung up over his right shoulder, the cord tangled under his arm and pressing at the back of his ear. The static and high pitched beep is becoming something to match his erratic heart and mind. He still senses Elijah's presence at the door and must commend his ability to stay there, outside, so quiet and still, waiting, and for what neither of them knows, Kal is only focused on his head, what he had needed so desperately to discuss with his father:

In his research for his book Kal had discovered that it was Daedalus who created one of the earliest labyrinths, on the island of Crete, to trap the Minotaur, and as legend has it he and his son Icarus were stuck there, on the island, and Daedalus devised the plan of creating wings made out of wax and feathers and did so, creating a viable means for the two to escape. Before they took flight Daedalus warned Icarus not to fly to close to the sun or the wax would melt. But Icarus, being the curious and naïve young man that he was did so anyway and fell into the ocean and drowned.

"Don't you think that's pretty potent considering what has happened today?" Kal would have said had his father called him back, "I find it interesting that these stories, the myth of centuries ago and the events unfolding there, today, both have to do with water and fathers and sons," which he was sure wasn't going to happen now. And even if it had his father would have been unable to comprehend all of this and would have said, "Really Kal, wings out of wax and feathers? You really think that would have worked, come on now!"

Kal would have been unable to correct his father, and would have hung up feeling no better.

This all would have happened had Kal's father called back but he hadn't and wasn't going to, Kal now knew. Kal, still with the receiver slung over his shoulder and pressed against his head and sensing Elijah's presence outside the door; Kal did the only thing he could do in that moment: laugh. He laughed so hard it seemed violent and forced, which it was after all, and when he thought about Elijah standing outside the door, listening with his ear pressed ever closer to the door to hear Kal's manic laugh he laughed harder, because he was sure that the muffling and distorting of his laughter through the door's wood made it sound, to Elijah, as if Kal were really crying, and maybe he was.

Eating Alone at Restaurants

I t doesn't happen the first time: the awkward little second glances and identifying and the whispers to other employees. These all come after say the third or fourth visit and we're not talking about a Denny's or a Steak & Shake or Waffle House or say even like a Taco Bell. The employees at these places could care less that you are there in the first place, let alone that you're coming back frequently and always alone. Not to mention the turnover rate at fast food joints and those 24 hour a day diner type places is so high it's hard to say who will be working there from week to week. It's the somewhat classier ones, the three and four star dine-in restaurants: The Cheesecake Factories and the Mongolian BBQs, and the Red Lobsters and places downtown where valets park your car if that's what you want. Just for the sake of argument lets also say that Applebee's and T.G.I.Fridays and maybe even Chili's are on the list since these are the nicer places around where he lives. He, being the subject: Melvin Shooley: 28 years old, lives alone, essentially an introvert; probably depressed, pudgy but not fat, not ugly but not exactly handsome either. He's neither too short nor too tall. Plain: is what people call him. He's just there, or isn't. He has the ability to stand in a crowded room and go unnoticed. He leaves and people say, "Melvin was here?" He rarely goes anywhere where he has to interact with a large herd of people his own age, instead spending all of his time in Barnes & Noble or the library, tucked away with his face between the covers of a book or else wandering the aisles like a lonely ghost.

Melvin Shooley works for a company that pays him minimum wage and expects maximum productivity with well managed stress over the increased workloads and fewer helping hands. He sits at a desk and moves things from one place to another. He makes telephone calls. He sends emails and photocopies reports to send to other people who photocopy said reports and send them to other people. Melvin goes to meetings every week in a conference room where a man tells him that times have been tough post-9/11 but are turning around and it's all thanks to sacrifice, hard work, and dedication. He, the man speaking, then asks the room to join him in chant-ing the company's theme song and give themselves a big round of applause for rebuilding America one double click at a time!

Melvin Shooley barely makes enough money each month at his job to cover rent, groceries, and gas. In fact, he doesn't make enough. He still borrows money almost weekly from his parents, which makes him feel totally worthless in terms of life. Any sort of hope he had at fulfillment in life is basically gone, and the possibility of one day falling in love seems impossible.

He's shy too, painfully so, and self-conscious. He didn't do any of the things you're supposed to do after high school, i.e. college, dating, and saving money work-ing a career in your field: marriage, and so on.

"Hope you've got a really bright plan you dumbass because one day you're going to be supporting me and your father's wrinkly old decrepit asses, loser," his mother said to him once while drunk, and: "try better fat ass, Jesus, how did I ever have a son who gained weight like it was his job… oh, I'm sorry Mel, I'm so sorry… I know you'll grow into the weight and be a very handsome young man and make some young lady very proud. I know you'll figure it out, you're so smart, now get some rest, and remember we love you, and jacking off is ok as long as you're thinking about girls," which makes Melvin sure that his phobias and neuroses are in part or whole due to his parents instability, both of them being closet alcoholics since Melvin was a little boy, functioning normally at mundane jobs where both of them made very good money but while at home the stress or unhappiness or whatever it was that drove them internally was too much to bear and so each had their alcoholic beverage of choice. Melvin's mother's was screwdrivers made with the cheap vodka that comes in a plastic jug. His father's: Schlitz's, 12-18 a night, with a shot of five acetaminophen to thin the blood beforehand. Then they'd fight, Melvin's mother and father, and when that was over they'd have sex so loud Melvin, as a teenager back then, would sometimes duct tape a pillow around his head, waking up in the morning with the tapes sticky residue irritating his skin and sometimes causing his forehead to break out.

It's no surprise that in school he was a loner, getting the shit beaten out of him constantly. His only friend being Sal ("Varg") Bologna, a Goth-type who wore eyeliner and got the shit beaten out of him even more than Melvin until his uncle signed him up for an intensive weekend long hand to hand combat, military funded, retreat which turned the tables entirely.

The worst part was Melvin wasn't even that smart. Most nerdy loner kids are like aspiring geniuses and advance quickly and don't struggle in the academic sense, but Melvin held down a C average and did nothing in the way of extracurricular activities. He basically just hung out with Sal and smoked weed and listened to Black Metal, which Sal said was only truly coming out of Norway and all the dumb American kids who wore corpse paint and black clothes were posers.

"These guys really practice what they preach," he told Melvin, "A lot of them are in jail for murder and rape and all kinds of shit. Others are dead, just killing themselves off. They're crazy. They don't just say things in songs to be dark and brooding, that's really just how they are."

Melvin never understood it. Sal wore black clothes and played music. In fact, after high school Sal hitch-hiked to LA to join a band called either 'Thoratic Death Cult' or 'Thoraxis' which he'd gotten hooked up with on MySpace and they were supposedly going to open for Skinny Puppy and Marilyn Manson on a North American tour, but things fell apart and Sal ended up back in Cleveland shortly thereafter, living with his mother and attending NA meetings for substance abuse he picked up in California. The meetings were in a church basement on Mondays and Thursdays. Sal had been working at a gas station; last Melvin had heard, and was still using a varietal cornucopia of substances, somehow continually avoiding testing through some maintained composure outside of his bedroom.

Ever since he'd come back things had changed be-tween them. Melvin still called him occasionally but they hadn't seen each other in quite some time. Mostly Melvin called to make sure Sal was doing OK and was alive. The conversations usually went like this: "Hey man, yeah... uh, hey... So, have you ever seen the movie Groundhog Day with Bill Murray, that thing....Ugh, Messed my world up man, seriously.... like, wow... The syntax in that thing, it's just... Jesus...fucked my entire world up let me tell you boy," Sal would say.

Melvin: "Cool, man, cool," ask how Sal had been do-ing.

Sal: "How am I doing? HA! How am I doing?... I'll tell you what man. Wake up. Ok? Just wake up... when the Reaper comes for my ass I'll be like, well... I'll be ready because, man, this is Hell. This day to day, so yeah Man."

Melvin: "Ok."

Sal is the reason Melvin is at least content enough in his own life to not want to use drugs. He even quit smoking weed because it made him paranoid and sick feeling.

These are the reasons Melvin Shooley eats alone at restaurants. Aside from just the obvious indications listed above (His parent's alcoholism, his psychotic drug addled best friend, nowhere job and bleak future, etc.) there is also the fact that at 28, Melvin has only ever kissed one girl, in the tenth grade, and the result was much apologizing and horrors Melvin doesn't even like to think about much less discuss at any length.

Melvin Shooley now lives in a studio apartment in the outskirts of the greater Cleveland area: a lesser known, slummier suburban city that was once flourishing in the post-World War Two prosperity but which as of late has been home to a shooting at a McDonald's just down the street from where Melvin lives, and a busted glory hole ring running out of four local Wal-Mart stores. His parents live in Maine. Melvin could live in Maine too but he decided to stay behind to keep his menial low paying office job.

The whole eating alone thing started when Melvin began going out late at night. He'd be up reading or something and he'd get hungry and there'd be no food in his apartment so he'd go to Denny's or a Wendy's just to get something. Sometimes he'd go to a Speedway and eat hot dogs off a roller oven. On Saturdays he might have stopped by Biagio's Donuts which was open until four am, get a coffee and a chocolate sprinkled donut as a late night snack. The whole thing became an experiment very quickly, though he didn't know the variables or what exactly he was hoping to achieve. He simply went somewhere and ate subpar food for cheap.

His trips to these kinds of places ended abruptly when one evening a clerk at a gas station, one whom Melvin had discoursed with before (both not remembering the other's name) asked Melvin if he, Melvin, wanted to see a photograph of his, the clerk's, baby, to which Melvin said sure and shrugged and the guy, the clerk, took out an aged polaroid, revealing to Melvin a picture of an AK-47, laid out on a bed, with the words: MY BABY AGE 2, written in the extra white space below the actual photograph.

It hadn't just been that one instance that stopped Melvin from going to his old haunts, he was looking to break with his normal patterns and routines, (that much became known about the experiment) and Melvin knew that if he was going to do that he'd have to start going places people would never expect to see a man his age dining alone on any night of the week. And so he began sometimes driving 20-30 miles to a restaurant to order a cheeseburger, fries, and a coke.

Sometimes he'd get exotic and order a rice dish, or Eggplant Parmesan, or something else he'd never had before. His new hobby was expensive but he liked it, and people did start to notice him: Managers, hostesses and hosts, waiters and waitresses, sometimes even the busboy or the cook would recognize him from a few nights previous or if he'd been in a week or two before (he stuck to no solid route, just going wherever he felt at that moment) and as odd as it was, these extra-long glances and the snickers and the whispers all created a tiny thread that Melvin felt connected him to these people, to others, which he hadn't known was the point at first but came to understand: What he was searching for was true companionship, not the kind based on some deep and abiding friendship, as he had with Sal, or the love of a significant other, but in the simplest form, under the pretense that he was a human being and everyone else in the room was a human being and in the end that should be enough for all of them. And it was enough for him, to have a waitress come over and smile and ask how he was doing and then take his order. It was enough to say maybe six words and then pay and leave; ending the transaction, not just of services and payments but of bodies occupying the same space and time, separately, and yet exchanging things deeper than any of them could comprehend as individuals going about their lives.

All of it became very exciting for Melvin who found he was thinking about things even when he wasn't experiencing them, as in at work or on the drive home or sitting alone at his apartment. He'd look at the car next to his and see a person he didn't know in the driver and passenger seat and think: We're connected and we (they) don't even know it. Sometimes he'd smile at someone who caught him looking and they'd either smile back or grimace and go back to staring at the light, waiting for it to change.

Overall the experience was changing Melvin and he felt happier, except in times when his own funds were running low and he was forced to call him parents whom he almost never did call unless he needed money and which just generally made him feel horrible and pathetic.

There is no reason for the parents of a 28 year old man to have his bank account number, he felt. But this was the Reality of the situation. Occasionally his mother would deposit money of her own volition. Other times Melvin would try and beat around the fact that he needed the money and in the morning wake up to find it'd been put there anyway, which usually made him cry, and after work he'd go out to get some Avocado Eggrolls which usually did the trick in sating his mind and readying him for the residual calls that were always bound to come. His parents called him regularly, usually after a couple screwdrivers and a sixer of Schlitz's. His father especially liked to call when on business trips, drunk of course on the hotel's minibar bottles, and tell Melvin all about his,

Melvin's father's, days in the ATF, working in conjunction with the United States Coast Guard, which Melvin's not sure he exactly believes but listened to anyway because it beat getting chewed out over something that had happened ten or 12 years earlier.

"Hi my name is Tabby, I'll be your server this evening, and can I start you off with something to drink?"

"A coke please," Melvin said.

The waitress left.

Melvin's phone rang. It was Sal.

"Hey," Melvin said.

"Hey yourself… Where the fuck have you been? I'm seriously having like this profound life experience over here, no shit. I've found the answer man, really and truly… They're all encoded in this god damn movie. I've watched it probably a hundred times now and each time I pick up on something new… I'm coming to a deeper und—"

"Whoa, whoa, whoa, slow down Sal, Jesus Christ… What are you talking about?"

"What do you think I'm talking about Dildo, the movie: Groundhog Day, with Bill Murray, hello? I've figured it out man and I need you to come by so I can show you all this shit because someone else needs to know about it, for real man. Seriously, so like: where the fuck are you?"

The waitress came back to the table and Melvin nodded at her. She was chewing gum. She stood there and blew a bubble then popped it with her teeth and walked away sucking the strip of gum off her chin.

"I'm really busy right now," Melvin said, putting a straw into his glass.

"Got you working overtime over there huh? Crunching data and shit, ha-ha, sucker! I've cracked the code of the world and all you do is dilly dally your bosses dick, man… What the fuck? This is pointless."

"What is?" Melvin asked, sipping his coke as quietly as he could.

"This talking to you, anyone, really… They won't get it, it's hard to understand."

"Well what exactly are you trying to get me to understand, Sal? You're not making it very easy for me here."

Sal laughed maniacally, "I thought I was making it pretty fucking clear myself."

"We–"

The line went dead.

The waitress came back over when she saw Melvin had put his phone down, "Were you ready to order?" She said, but he only looked up at her as if he were worried, and picked up his phone again, "Sorry," he said, to the waitress, and dialed the Bologna's house number, which he somehow still remembered.

The waitress left again, sighing as she parted.

The Bologna's phone rang, "Hello?" A woman's voice said from the other end.

"Hi, Mrs. Bologna, this is Melvin," Melvin said.

"Oh hi, Melvin, how are you? It's been quite some time since I've seen you."

"I'm good, busy, staying very busy… Is Sal around?"

"He's in his room. He's been writing new music. I'll go grab him for you, one se—"

"Actually," Melvin said, "Mrs. Bologna, I was hoping to talk to you for a second,"

"Oh," she said. "Well what is it you'd like to talk to me about?"

"I guess I'm just wanting to get your perspective on Sal, I mean is he doing better than he was?"

"Oh Heaven's yes. He's much much better... He's writing music again! And engaging me and reading books... It's so wonderful to see him active and alert and responding to things."

"That's good," Melvin said, feeling saddened in the way hearing good things about people you care about when you've been at a distance from that person is liable to make anyone feel sad, "And he's still going to meetings and that sort of thing?"

"Uh-huh, I drive him myself," Mrs. Bologna said, "Melvin are you sure you wouldn't like to speak to Sal he's just in his room it'd be no trouble at all to go and get him for you?"

"No that's alright," Melvin said, "I just wanted to hear from you that he was alright. He had sounded like he... Well, he was probably just being the old prankster Sal Bologna that he is. Sorry to bother you Mrs. Bologna."

"Oh it's no bother at all Melvin, You know Sal, always the joker," Mrs. Bologna said, "Was there anything else?"

"No that's it, goodnight Mrs. Bologna."

"Goodnight then Melvin." She said and hung up.

A week passed.

Melvin went in and out of work feeling the way he imagined it felt being on a train passing through a tunnel: for a second nothing happens, all conversations cease and it's as if people hold their breath, wondering whether they'll come out the other side; totally dark. Outside work was just the same. He went from place to place and kept coming in and out of lucidity. At one point he found himself standing in the middle of the parking lot at Giant Eagle with no idea how he'd got there or what he was doing, then he remembered where he parked and drove home.

Currently he is in Fat Fish Blue, a southern style jazz influenced restaurant on the corner of Prospect and Ontario in the heart of Downtown, enjoying the soulfulness of the trumpeter leading the live band and a gumbo dish he's not even sure the correct pronunciation of, which doesn't matter at all to him as he eats, feeling good, really good for the first time since he called Mrs. Bologna. He was just worried about Sal. Thought about going to see him but decided against it. He didn't know what he'd say or do, it'd been so long.

His cell phone rings. It's his mother. He answers it.

"Hello," he says.

There is a pause, then he hears static and fragments of gargled speech, "Mom?" he says, but the call is lost... "Damn," he says, standing up from his booth, dialing back her number. It goes straight to voicemail. "Fu–"

He's outside, pacing, waiting for his mother to call him back.

The screen lights up.

"Hello," he says without even looking at it, "Hello, mom?"

"Melvin?" a woman's voice that is not his mother's says, sniffling, shakily.

"Who is this?"

"It's Mrs. Bologna, Melvin," the voice says.

"Mrs. Bologna, I'm sorry but I'm waiting for a very important call from my mother right now. She's actually trying to call now, hold on…" He says and switches lines, "Mom? Mom?"

"Melvin?… What the hell is going on?"

"I don't know something with the phones, what's wrong?"

"I'm leaving your father Melvin." His mother says.

"What? What are you talking about?"

She burst into tears, "He's been cheating on me… The bastard, He's been fucking that Wendy Poppenstove in Canada all along. I've emptied one of the accounts. I'm heading back to Cleveland tomorrow morning. I just thought you should know."

"Hold on," Melvin says, "What are you talking about?"

"I just told you Melvin, your father is fucking cheating on me. I found out the other day. I was playing Minesweeper on his laptop like I like to do, you remember, and I ended up accidentally going through his email and found an entire correspondence between him and that Wendy Poppenstove woman from Canada and it's all about…. Well, I won't go into details but its," She cries harder, "He's fucking her."

Something was falling through Melvin with great weight and speed.

"But—"

"You're god damn right but, he's a liar, a fucking asshole. God…. How could I not know, for all this time how did it happen without me catching on? I mean there are times when we're physical that—"

"Mom!" Melvin yells.

"Sorry sorry, it's just… Oh, I don't know. I just feel so stupid. Like a stupid little child."

A large black man in an all-black suit barrels through the door of Fat Fish Blue and glances quickly around, spotting Melvin and pointing at him as if daring him to move, which Melvin doesn't, realizing he hadn't paid the bill and simply left. He puts up a finger signaling for the guy to hold on just one sec, then he tells his mother that he has to call her back in the morning, which she doesn't hear because she is smashing an ice tray into the counter top and screaming something at the top of her lungs in some other direction than the phones mic.

Melvin hangs up, "Sorry," he says to the black man, and follows him back inside to pay his check.

On the drive home his cell phone rings again. It's his father, "What has she said Melvin?… What are the accusations? I need to know son, right now. She's emptied one of the bank accounts and is not here, she just took off. Screamed something and sped away with a screwdriver… She's totally drunk and driving and upset, so what did she say? Tell me, for the love of God please right now, just tell me son."

Melvin sighs. He doesn't feel like talking anymore.

"Is it true?" He asks his father.

"Is what true? I am unaware of the accusations so how can I either deny or confess? I don't know what is going on as of right now, that's why I need you to tell me, to spit it out. I need information. I need data. I need to know: What does she believe, what–"

Melvin's cell's screen lights up and out of the corner of his eye he sees it and thinking it's his mother he says, "Hold on dad," and switches over.

It's not his mother. It's Mrs. Bologna again.

"I'm sorry I haven't called you back Mrs. Bologna, I guess—"

"Melvin," Mrs. Bologna says somberly, and then pauses. She is audibly crying into the phone and Melvin had seen enough movies to know what was coming next. He didn't consciously think that exact thought but felt it in his heart, like a pin poke, then a stab. His whole chest tightens up and Mrs. Bologna sits quietly weeping into the phone and Melvin feels tears in his own eyes as he involuntarily pulls the car off the road and sits with the caution lights on.

"Sal," he finally says after minutes of silence, and Mrs. Bologna's nod is almost audible as her weeping becomes more pronounced and she apologizes and says, "You sensed it didn't you? That's why you called…" a sigh, "I-um, he was… Oh god…" She says, "How cou—"

Melvin's cell keeps lighting up as he sits for another few minutes in silence, Mrs. Bologna sobbing and saying little things to herself more so than to Melvin. Melvin is just there to act as… well he doesn't exactly know what, retainer, maybe? He himself is crying but not nearly enough and soon Mrs. Bologna composes herself to tell Melvin the details of the wake and that she's sorry and that if he needs anything call her, and he says the same to her, and they hang up. Cars zip by at light speed. Melvin sits there on the shoulder for a minute and everything blurs then takes it shape again. His body feels heavy. Every movement feels to him as if it's being made in a pool of molasses. He thinks: The world is Molasses, and when he thinks about smiling at how dumb this thought is he just starts crying more because his best friend is dead and he wasn't there to even try and save him and now there is nothing anyone can do.

Sal is simply gone.

His phone doesn't stop ringing the whole way home.

In the morning he calls work and tells them he won't be in for a few days. They don't ask why and he doesn't tell them. He imagines they know. That everyone knows and this is there consolation, not asking questions. His parents don't call him for two or three days. It's he who will finally call them, but until then he lays in bed in boxers and a t-shirt and stares at the ceiling fan whirling around or else it's the television screen with a DVD playing that he's not interested in watching but lets it go on a loop until he falls back asleep.

He doesn't eat.

Even thinking about eating anything at all feels like committing a grave sin and so he lives off water from the tap, cupped in a hand, for two days. Eating feels like the cause of Sal's death. If Melvin hadn't been going on those stupid fucking adventures to restaurants all by himself he could have maybe spent time with Sal and possibly even saved him, showed him he needed more help, talked him into getting serious about rehab or something. He could have done something. But he didn't, he brushed it off with overpriced food and now what?

The wake happens.

Sal always wanted to be cremated so there's only the wake. It's held at a local funeral parlor and is open casket. Sal looks like a badly painted version of himself. His skin dry and flaky with makeup, hair combed (which it never was), and he's in a suit. Personal items placed by the family rest near him in the casket: photographs, guitar picks, a Dimmu Borgir t-shirt, copies of books that he loved. Melvin has nothing to put in. He stands at the casket and tries not to cry but the realization that Sal was once a person and his best friend sets in and he's unable to fight. Mrs. Bologna hugs him and everyone in the room feels the exact same thing that Melvin feels, even in terms of the guilt, asking themselves what they could have done to foresee it and stop him from doing it.

Melvin had called his parents and told them what was going on and they said they were sorry and that they would come as soon as they could but that it wouldn't be for the wake and that they were sorry too for getting Melvin all worried the same night he found out because his parents, they said, "…decided not to fight anymore, and that the past is the past and we're going to get help, counseling; really this time and work things out and stay together and it will be so much better," They said, "We're so sorry about Sal. We know you two were close."

He said, "Shut the fuck up,"

And his mother said, "What?"

And he said, "Shut the fuck up shut the fuck up shut the fuck uuuuppppp!!!" and hung up, and turned his phone off.

He'd agreed to have dinner with Mrs. Bologna sometime that week. He skipped the post-wake gathering at her house and instead drove down to a bar he and Sal used to sneak into as underage kids and drink the half empties, usually getting caught and told to fuck off before the police came, which they really relished, laughing about it and feeling cool and telling the stories of their debauchery to girls at school dances in hopes of making out with them or at least slow dancing, instead ditching early to smoke a joint behind the school before Mrs. Bologna picked them up.

Melvin ordered a beer and sat dejectedly at the bar. A football game was on the television, he watched it with a kind of detached numb hum in his head and occasionally looked around at all the other people in the room, not feeling much of anything, his epiphanies and the whole eating alone experiments felt as though they were part of a past life and had happened a million years before.

He had a few more drinks, time rolled on.

He goes back to work.

Then comes the day he and Mrs. Bologna had agreed to have dinner and he meets her at the restaurant, one he is quite familiar with.

She looks better and he hugs her and they go inside. A hostess seats them and says a waitress will be right over.

Melvin thanks her.

After a few minutes of silence while sitting at the table Mrs. Bologna perks up and says, "Oh," reaching into her purse to retrieve something: a folded envelope, which she slides across the table to Melvin, already tearing up by time he takes it in his hand and glances at it and knows, and moves over to her side of the table and puts his arm around her and tells her it's ok, squeezing her shoulder and telling her it is going to be alright.

"This is, uh… This is—" Melvin begins but can't think of what to say. His mind goes blank and he just sits there squeezing Mrs. Bologna's shoulder and rocking with her a little as her chest heaves with sadness.

The waitress comes over, sees the scene, and mouths the word sorry. Melvin, having read the apology off her lips, puts up a hand as if to say: its ok, not your fault. He's been saying this lot knowing full well it's not ok, not really, nothing is. The waitress is his age and her name tag reads: Marcy. He looks at her as she stands there. It probably all occurs in a matter of twenty seconds but she stands there and he looks at her, stares really, and Mrs. Bologna sniffles and looks at Melvin and he looks at her and he can see she's shedding some of the weight of the thing right there at that table and he feels like maybe he is too, in some way he can't even describe. He feels a bit of the weight come off his own chest and looks back at the waitress, Marcy, and she's still there, not to be rude or force them to order or anything but just making sure everything is alright, and without saying a word Melvin nods but doesn't smile, knowing why she's still there, and she smiles, not in a flirtatious or cute way, with teeth and everything. It's more one of those little doubtful but very meaningful smiles where there's nothing to say but what she means is, *I understand.*

Warfield

I t was always the same if he asked his mother: she'd get hysterical crying and jog out of whatever room she was in with her hand over her mouth; closing herself off in her room for sometimes the rest of the day and night, which naturally made him feel like it was his fault, whatever it was, and he'd end up sobbing in his own room and feeling bad for asking in the first place. So he just didn't ask her anymore, and if he found himself thinking about his father he might say offhandedly to his brother something like: "When dad punched that mirror that one time, the one in the bathroom, you know when you lost your tooth and he walked in as it slipped out of your fingers and went cherplunk in the toilet water, he must have lost a heckuva lotta blood if he passed out right there." Or: "When he had you digging those holes in the backyard and he wouldn't tell you why, what do you think he was doing?"

Toby was seven years older than Samuel and knew their father. Toby was the only one who'd had substantial contact with the man since his brother was born only a year and a half before he, their father, walked out of the house and never came back, leaving their mother and Toby and his brother, Samuel (more so Samuel), to wonder: what made him disappear all of a sudden; not the final act, but the underlying causes and their effects, and why wouldn't he want to talk to either of his sons at least?

"His brain was fried." Toby said, late one night when Samuel snuck into his room, unable to sleep with all the thoughts in his head and the bird not helping any,

"In forty-four we moved from Texas to Utah, to a new army base. That's when things got real bad. This was when he had me digging the holes in the backyard for no reason. He'd say, 'Toby I want this hole to be three feet wide and three feet deep and I want it right here,' and he'd point to a spot. 'And I want it done by time I get back,' he'd say and then he'd leave. He was gone all the time, wouldn't talk to anyone when he was home. I remember he always looked like he was really deep in thought, like he was keeping a world full of secrets that would never come out, at least not to us... But one time mom got something caught in the sink drain, maybe a towel or something, I don't remember, but she had to call someone over to fix it and the guy that came didn't have a clue what he was doing. It was actually quite funny to watch, especially now that I know what was happening, it's funny in a sad way, maybe. I don't know. Dad was toast. Mom and dad got in a big fight and after that mom stopped talking for a while too."

"What was the fight about?"

"If you must know: when we got to the base there was an exorbitant amount of—"

"What's that?" Samuel asked

"What's what?"

"Exor-ba-tent?" Samuel said.

"Exorbitant, it's like, well… It was just there was a lot more people there than normal, on the base, and when we got there mom asked what was going on because we'd been living on army bases practically forever and she'd never seen that many people around and dad told her they were all sanitary workers, which seemed a bit absurd probably to any rational person who understood the base didn't need that many sanitary workers and anyway they weren't. They were theorists and physicists."

"What are those?"

"They're people who are really smart but so smart that sometimes they're dumb and do things that hurt people, or in this case, let's just say they didn't make house calls, ha ha, let's just say that… So when mom called one of these guys over to the house to fix the sink drain, it's funny in its sad little way because here's this genius who knows about all these big ideas but who doesn't know how to unclog a sink drain, and he was absolutely baffled." Toby said.

His brother didn't laugh. "So dad lied?"

"About everything squirt, every god da- all of it, and mom only found out after the fact. I mean she had her ideas and her and dad were always fighting, but really it didn't all come into light until after he did what he did and it wasn't secret anymore and then it all blew up and he left, because before that dad and all his friends were the only ones who knew what was going on, really, and but then she and the whole world knew and dad was everywhere, or not so much him but what he and his friends had done,"

"What did they do again, I forget?"

"You didn't forget dummy, I never told you, and I never will."

"Why Toby, why won't you just tell me, I'm not a kid anymore, I can handle it, I want to know." Samuel pleaded.

Toby shook his head, "Too bad. Someday you will know, but you're too young to understand. Enjoy being a kid. Now go read and get to bed, it's late and I'm tired."

"I'm not tired though." His brother said eagerly. "Tell me something else."

"It's too late squirt, go to bed and we'll talk tomorrow."

"Come on! Please, just one more small thing and then I'll go to bed I swear."

Toby sighed, "Fine," he said, adjusting himself in the bed: "We'd all been invited by dad's bosses and friends to see a movie. You were still a baby so you couldn't come so mom and dad got a babysitter for you. The movie was a movie based on what dad and his friends did. It was a special screening just for the families and people involved or something, so it was more of an honorary thing for dad and his friends, and mom didn't want to go. She made it clear she didn't want to go. I think she hated him by this point. But we all went and sat through this movie and had to stand around while dad talked to people... It was really boring and made me feel sad and mom too, and when we got in the car she started crying. They argued the whole way home and mom cried the entire time and I think I probably cried too and they kept fighting after I'd been sent to bed; I didn't hear much of it but the next morning when we were all having breakfast dad called me 'little boy' or something, in some way mom didn't like one bit and mom hauled off and smacked him hard on the cheek and he grabbed her and flung her to the floor by her arm and then walked out of the house, and that's the last time we saw him. He didn't take his clothes or anything. He just left. I'm telling you: he was totally fried like an egg, squirt; gone. Probably from what he did. But anyway you were up in your crib asleep and mom just sat on the floor and I sat at the table looking at her and she was looking at me and dad was gone. Everyone left at the house was frozen in time, or something, like in a movie," Toby said, and then: "Now go to bed, I've said enough about it tonight."

"Do you ever miss him?" Samuel asked.

"Go to bed, now." Toby said, pushing his brother off the edge of the bed and forcing him to start the walk to his room.

Samuel had a tiny bird his mother had bought him for his birthday. They'd always fascinated him, birds had, and when he watched them it helped him become aware of something he wasn't aware of before, though he didn't know what that meant. He liked the way they flocked together, the way they flew in patterns, or all sat perched on the feeder, together, as one. Maybe that's what he became aware of: how bad he wanted everyone to be together again.

In the cage though the bird was alone and was boring, it just stood on its dumb rod and made idiotic sounds that when Samuel listened to them for too long they became really annoying and made Samuel want to release it out the window, into its natural habitat, which he never would do, but thought about doing several times.

He kept the bird because on nights that he wondered about things, like his dad and what he had done or where he was or what he was doing at that exact moment or why he left just out of the blue and with nothing, not even clothes or a toothbrush, he'd stare at the bird in its cage and sometimes that would make it easier for him to drift off to sleep, staring at the bird, or if not he'd watch it, that dumb little bird in its dumb little cage, pecking at its feathers or singing its dumb little song, and his brain would switch over to a new thought, not about why Toby had to dig holes or why his dad punched the bathroom mirror but instead about why the bird did the things it did and what the reason was, if there was any, for it to do those things in the first place.

Facsimiles or,

a Modern Tale of Romance

2: something (as an extravagant story or account) that lacks basis in fact.

I watched her for hours a day; it was her job to be watched. My own work took the backseat to my watching her. Her doing anything, it wasn't just a sexual voyeurism. She could be sitting on the couch eating a bowl of cereal, cooking dinner, or preparing for bed. It didn't matter what she did I was there, and so were the others. We were all there together, watching and waiting for the next moment, the next surprise. What would she do? The webcam followed her like a well-trained pet. It captured everything, life as it was being lived there in her apartment, and I could not take my eyes away from the screen. Each month I diligently paid the renewal fee for my membership to her site, her feed. It was like a trough, and it only cost twenty-two dollars for unlimited access to a real life, Mathilda's life.

We were all willing to pay.

Before I disabled the chat feed it showed over a hundred current members, all of them incognizant, shielded behind monikers bestowed on them by the rules of the game. Characters and numbers, that's all they were; and they sent a dizzying amount of messages, requests and provocations. They were dogs in a kennel, tearing at each other. Sometimes Mathilda felt compelled to respond; throw them a bone. She'd flash a breast or pull her panties up into the crease of her crotch. Even that wasn't enough. They wanted to see her fucking herself with a dildo or straddling a chair arm completely naked and glistening with baby oil. They'd come to expect a lot from the internet's projection but she was a real girl, a person with a life. They couldn't understand the privilege of simply being there, being able to peek in on her doing the most mundane thing. They didn't receive the gift they were given. They wanted more, *more*, and would leap into the vile and profane. And sometimes Mathilda would masturbate for us, laying herself up in bed with her fingers crawling below the covers. She allowed us in to this sensuous act that was not the least bit pornographic; the rustling of the comforter, the quivering of her shoulders as she came; the moans. If I turned up the volume on my computer's speakers I could hear the shakiness in her breath as she released her inner flood. I'd think about that as I brought myself to climax, there in the chair. It didn't take long, eyes closed, fantasy reel running. Audible whispers from Mathilda there with me, really there, delighting in my thrusts, in my girth.

In the shower afterwards I'd imagine what it would be like if I actually found her, if we bumped into each other on the street or in a store, just happened upon the other somewhere. What would that be like? Or what if I found out where she lived; set it up so that I met her in a purely coincidental seeming fashion. Hey wow, you're Mathilda. I'm a member! You come to Whole Foods too?

Would that be awkward or would it seem like fate? Would she even find me attractive? Would she respond to flirtation? Could she date someone like me, with all my insecurities and neuroses?

The questions sometimes consumed me and I found it hard to sleep. I'd max out the speakers and listen to her rhythm, her REM cycle, try to match it, or I'd sit up and stare at her through the pixilated window, try to put myself next to her, astral project myself into her bed: hover above her, like a ghost, disembodied and feeling her warmth through the pure static of my ethereal presence, feeling it in my deepest parts, in my essence.

I'd pass out and wake up to find her sitting at the kitchen table, reading the *New Yorker*, eating a protein bar, laughing with such a childlike innocence at the cartoons it echoed with profundity.

At work I'd have her feed pulled up in a background window and watch during lulls in customer calls. At the peak of the afternoon she usually did some yoga or went out for a walk. The camera never followed into the outside world, it stayed at her desk where she'd post a note explaining what she was doing, where she was, and when she would be back. She never left us without word.

Mathilda was also an artist. Some days I'd pull up the window to find her working on a painting, large abstract works she'd had great success in showing and selling. I visited the gallery websites and could scroll through thumbnails of her oeuvre. Some had sold for over two thousand dollars. Her presence on the internet was greatly affecting other aspects of her life and I realized that although she was there, with me and with us, all of us, she was also out *there*, in the world, doing things that made her a much more interesting and mysterious person. What I saw was just a fraction of what made her *her*, she had depths I could never know or imagine. She was realer than real, both present and yet absent, like the deity of Christ bound to flesh and bone. I'd watch her bring the brush down on the canvas. It seemed to move her more than she moved it. Nothing she did felt rehearsed, an effect you sometimes have watching 'reality' television or documentary films. It made me want to do *more*, inspired me I guess. There she was, unafraid of who she was and what she did; confident and sure in every way. How could I not feel the draw? How could I not want to try and reach her level of existence, wouldn't that bring me closer to her, in spirit? Mathilda was the realest human being I've ever known and yet she remained, for all that I knew of her, an abstraction. We stayed at a distance, despite her filling my consciousness and informing my decisions.

At times, with all the other windows closed out and the chat bar minimized, Mathilda would fill the screen, the frame, and it felt like she'd somehow filled me, entered me through some portal and we were the only two people in existence, melded together through the high speed connectivity and 1080hp resolution, suspended in the ether, the void.

Mathilda never used her feed as a blog. She wouldn't sit and chat with us. She was simply recording her life. She wasn't there to advertise anything. It was a source of income, sure, but it wasn't a career. The world had forged her this way and she was simply doing all that she knew how to do. We responded to it. She didn't care for us the way we, I, cared for her. How could she, she didn't know any of us, not the way we knew her. Not the way I did.

No.

I didn't expect her gaze to meet mine through the distance of our separate screens. That would defy the laws of the Universe and as much as I wish it were possible some things are forbidden.

Things went on just as they had, only I found myself devising ways of recording Mathilda's feed, taking the 'real' to reproduction. Not for pleasure, but for study. Mathilda deserved that, whether she knew it or not. I thought about setting up a camera in front of my computer and doing it that way but that would mean that I would have had to miss out on the viewing and substitute it with a second hand sitting. That would have diminished the magic of the moments, of being there with her, and I couldn't have that. That was the whole point of the viewing in the first place. To be there with her, as things happened, that's what mattered. The recordings were to be a reference, a guide, not an end but a means of bringing catharsis.

The revelation came to me at an electronics store. I was there buying new toner for my boss's copier and printer. I stumbled upon add-on software for a webcam that allowed users to invert the recording option using both a newly formatted system application and a special reflective lens. It only cost a hundred dollars so I bought it and went back to the office, told my boss someone had rear ended me and that I needed to take the rest of the day off to go to urgent care and get checked out.

"It's my neck," I said.

My boss was a sucker and a worry wart. Since technically I wasn't supposed to be off the premises while on the clock and he should have been going to the store to get supplies he told me to take the rest of the day off and call him when I knew if I'd need more time. He didn't even tell me to make sure to bring back a note. He just let me go.

I left the building smiling and drove home with the package in the passenger seat. It was barely able to contain itself to the point I had to put my hand down over it to physically restrain it until I got it back to my apartment and could start the install.

Mathilda was at lunch with her mother. She hated her mother. She'd let us in on several phone conversations and it was obvious that she and her mother were not the best of friends. He mother didn't approve of Mathilda's 'lifestyle' choices and Mathilda liked to end these talks quickly, with a lot of screaming at both ends and absolutely no resolution.

Sometimes she had her cell phone on speaker.

She wouldn't even deny us the opportunity to eaves drop; in fact she insisted that we did.

The install took about an hour. I was unable to access the terminal during this time. The lens was an easy piece to attach to the already existing lens on the webcam. All there was to do after that was wait. I tried to call forth out of the abyss where Mathilda and her mother were eating and what she, Mathilda, was wearing. What had she ordered? What kind of foods did she eat at restaurants? Were Mathilda and her mother arguing? What about? Was there something I didn't know about?

There was a moment of panic when the idea that maybe she was pregnant popped into my head. She'd been seeing a guy, Bradley, on and off at the start of the feed but he, like her mother, didn't approve of the lifestyle and stopped coming around. He was an asshole of the highest caliber. But, I thought, what if when one of the times Mathilda had left a note like: Dealing with Bradley again! UGH! Or Don't ask, seriously, she'd somehow slept with him, gotten suckered into it or was drunk and let him have his way with her one more time, out of guilt or something. What would that say about her? What if he'd raped her or something and she was too afraid to come out and say it? Was that why she'd been wearing all those loose fitting dresses? Was she showing?

Luckily none of this was the case. She was still herself, perfect. She allowed us in to even her deepest moments.

The first recording I made was of her crying after the lunch with her mother. She curled herself up in a blanket on her bed and quietly wept. Later I opened up the chat bar just to see if she'd maybe hinted at what had happened, what was wrong. What I found was:

C@S3B0742: Wat's wrong bay-bay?

Mathilda@home: Sometimes life makes me feel like a failure.

Ran5tar*69: pic or it did not happen.

C@S3B0742: Youll be ok. Youre a smart bee-u-t-full talented young grl with a bright future ahead of you. Keap yo head up :)

TonytheN!5: Show your tits! Show your tits! Show your tits!

DoomBoxSup: ^ wat he said.

Mathilda@home: Thanks C@S3B0742!!! : D

Ran5tar*69: Pussy.

TonytheN!5: Casebots a faggot.

Nobius33: Yep, sure is. Faggot faggot faggot faggot.

I thought about typing out a long winded apology and expressing empathy for her situation but the bar just kept scrolling and scrolling so fast it would have been pointless.

In the weeks that proceeded I began my studies. What I was looking for were elements of Mathilda's life I could bring into my own, easily accessible parts or items I could purchase that would make me feel closer to her: a red-wood bedside table from Pier One Imports, a bookcase from Ikea, Target Bed sheets, a second hand store writers desk (I found one at a thrift store that was a near perfect match), a MacBook, art supplies from Utrecht, A body pillow from Bed, Bath, & Beyond. There were the small-er, more inconspicuous things: the aloe vera hand lotion from Bath & Body Works, Abercrombie and Fitch perfume (not to wear, only to spray around my apartment to create the idea that she had been there), a pair of Love Pink sweatpants, Dove body wash, Three Olives Cherry Vodka, Sprite in 20oz bottles, and a Catholic Feast of St. Francis candle (Ironic?).

I'd started calling off work more and more, elaborating on my original lie.

"Tests," I'd say to my boss, "they want to be sure there's no ligament damage." Or: "They found something in my blood, an abnormality. They want me to come back in tomorrow for more blood work and a CT scan."

By the end of that December he'd caught on and the day he called me into his office to 'talk' I knew what was coming and went in guns blazing, not literally of course, figuratively.

"B—"

"I have cancer," I said.

"What?" He couldn't tell if he'd heard me incorrectly or if I'd said what he heard or if I'd even spoken at all. He looked instantly haunted.

I went on to explain in brilliant detail my illness. I even brought myself to tears there in his office and he got out of his chair and hugged me. I couldn't help but laugh and masked it by crying harder, more violently.

As I was exiting his office to begin my medical leave he said, "If you need anything, anything at all. Don't hesitate to call."

"Thanks," I said, feigning a feigned smile.

At home I described the exploit to the Fridge. It was now full of organic beverages and Whole Foods bought condiments. I sat at the kitchen table, facing the Fridge.

"Now I've got all the time in the world!" I said.

"That's nice," the Fridge said back. It sounded a lot like Eeyore from the Winnie the Pooh cartoons I'd watched as a child.

"Why do you seem more glum than usual?" I asked the Fridge, "this is a great day to be alive!"

"I don't have any feelings. I am what I am because of what you put into me," it said, "Otherwise I'd just be a cold box."

"We'll have to work on that," I said.

"Ok," the Fridge said dejectedly.

That night there was a note from Mathilda: New Hope?!?! XOXO

What was that supposed to mean? I wondered. Where was she?

It was late.

This had always been one of the major hurdles of the exchange. If she was away then I had no idea where she was or what was happening. What if she was hurt, or worse? What if she was being held at knife point? There'd have been nothing I could do with her sometimes cryptic notes. New Hope? What the… What the fuck?

That night I drove around and looked for her. I wasn't sure where she lived but I figured if it was in the area I'd find her. It was possible. Stranger things have happened you know. It is a small world after all. But I had no luck spotting her. She was vapor. She was mist. She was a heavenly body. She did not exist.

I stopped in at a bar and thought I'd maybe just have a couple drinks while I waited for her to return. I ended up really drunk and enmeshed in a doozy of a conversation with a girl half my age that ended up in my bed asking me: "Do you have a girlfriend? That's so hot! Is she going to come home? Does she eat pussy? That'd be so hot?"

I put my hand over her mouth and got rough. She liked it. I hadn't drunk that much in a long time and my cock felt like a string bean. I fell off of the girl and passed out. Woke up oblivious to what had happened. The girl was in my kitchen making eggs.

"Hey!" She said, "Where's your girlfriend? Is she coming home? I'll cook extra."

"That was a… That was a mistake, last night," I said, leaning into the counter.

"No such thing."

"I don't have a girlfriend," I said, "But I am in love with a girl."

"No such thing."

I ate the eggs she cooked and then told her she had to leave, "I have a lot of work to do," I told her.

She kissed me and left me her number.

When she was out in the hall and the door was locked I cried and fell into a wall.

"Who was that?" the Fridge asked.

"Don't ask," I said sniffling.

"I already did," the Fridge said.

"She was nobody," I said, "Worst of all that meant nothing. I don't know her name. She wasn't a good Mathilda facsimile. You wouldn't know about this but this is the way those types of arrangements work. It's just two people looking for someone in the other person they know they're not going to find. It's sad really. I'm just very sad."

The Fridge said nothing else.

Out of shame I stayed away from the computer. I showered for longer than was usual, scrubbed harder, and left my skin scorched by the loofa. I ate a small meal at lunch. The cabinets had begun to put in their two cents, mumbling: scumbag, scumbag, scumbag…

"I know!" I screamed, "I know, just please just leave me alone."

"I wasn't even saying anything," the Fridge said.

"Not you," I said.

"Then who?"

Ignoring the Fridge I moved to the living room and turned on the television. *Fantom or Phantom?*, one of the only programs I could stand to watch anymore, was having a marathon so I decided to watch, more consumed it. The next time I glanced at a clock it'd been hours, literally having fell off the day. I felt well enough to return to the computer, to gaze upon Mathilda once more, whatever she was doing. I could hear the Fridge whispering something in the background.

"Shut up!" I screamed across the apartment.

There was silence.

Mathilda was still absent. In her place was a new note: *Maybe?*

Maybe what?

I downloaded the material that had been recorded from the previous night up until that moment, parsed it for clues to what Maybe? meant, and that's when I noticed it: In the room: two shadowy forms moving through the dark. Two: Mathilda had not been alone either. That's what the *maybe* signified, having an attachment outside of the arrangement she'd made with us, her viewers. Mathilda had been the object of our collective affection but I had betrayed it and she followed suit. The forms hovered above the bed. It was impossible for me to watch and not feel sick, sick for myself and my actions and sick for what was there, set in stone, drawn out of real life and set to record. There, right there. In the live feed she was still absent, the note stood there tormenting me: Maybe? Maybe? Maybe?

The Eternal Question.

I needed my head to shut off, my head or the world, whichever came first.

I went back to the living room, stomped there on feet that felt caked in mud, and turned on the television. The marathon was still running but I couldn't watch. I channel surfed through day time talk shows, commercials, soap operas, and reality shows. I stopped on an advertisement for a product claiming to be able to remove every follicle of hair from a human's body through laser augmentation. All of the dramatization actors had perfectly sculpted and hairless bodies: All yours for only $19.95 w/S&H.

The erection made itself known.

I had to get out.

I threw on some clothes and fled.

Up the street from my apartment there was a large box retailer bookstore with connected coffee shop. I'd go there when I felt like I needed to be a part of the world but didn't want to get to close, when things got to heavy at home. The Fridge could really get on my nerves. Sometimes I'd try and pick up an orange that would end up weighing as much as a shot-put ball. Everything was messing with me.

Now there was the Mathilda dilemma. The revealing of my own soul's wretchedness had somehow transferred itself to her as well, possibly through the radio waves and signals sent from my router. She'd gone to the Shadow at the same instant I myself had given myself over to the girl from the bar. These events were locked in a kind of parabolic state. I could see it all at my vantage and it drove me nearly insane. It took a few punches of the steering wheel of my car, leaving streaks of white dead skin on the rubber, just to be able to walk into the building. The fluorescent lights harsh glow caught me off guard and I nearly fell into a display for the latest James Patterson bestseller but caught myself and acclimated to the light and my rage and self-incriminations melted with the smooth bass line of an aged jazz song playing through the speakers.

I walked contemplatively from section to section, my head filled with musings about the world and myself and all of mankind: light, music, and the voices of others in conversations about who knew what. It all mingled and sang with the world and I felt light, buoyant. I glided on butterfly wings to the counter of the café. In front of me was a younger couple. They were happy. I was feeling happy. I watched them there, flirting and being quite indecisive about what to order. They'd turned it into a game.

"What do you want?" the guy asked.

"I don't know. What are you getting?" the girl asked back.

"I don't know either, just order." The guy said laughing.

"I don't know what I want though," the girl said.

The guy sighed playfully, "It's not that hard," he said.

"Well then just order for me," the girl said.

"What am I?" the guy asked.

"You're the man." The girl said.

"Damn right," the guy said with a smirk, "now what do you want?"

"I don't know!" The girl shrieked.

They did finally order. I stood there smiling pleasantly as I waited for the barista to prepare and serve their drinks. I waited for the barista, who was a middle aged woman in a black top and apron, to come back to the register and take my order.

"Hi," she said, "What can I get for you?"

I looked over her head at the menu hung up on the wall behind her. I tried to look as if I were thinking hard about what I wanted, weighing options, and changing my mind. "Hmmm," I said, rubbing my chin. I wanted to look absolutely human. Normal, totally supposed to be there doing what I was doing.

The barista never got annoyed or sighed; at least she didn't show it.

I took my time.

I said, "Umm," and paused, then: "I'll have *a*..." I stammered. I felt my face sag and my tongue fall out of my mouth. Out of my stomach arose guttural sounds I made no effort to produce. My whole body tightened up. The barista kept her eyes on me, never looking embarrassed or concerned. I kept my eyes on her, focusing as best I could. We were looking at each other, or rather, I was looking at her but she did not see me.

Reflection

He went into the bathroom one day when he was very young and his father was in there shaving. The door had been cracked so he just pushed and there was his old man lathered up with the razor to his cheek. When his father saw him he smiled and with one arm swooped the child up and sat him on the edge of the sink so that he could watch as his old man brought the razor down with smooth even strokes, "Just like cutting the lawn," His father joked, winking at the child. His father's neck was splotchy and red and the child didn't quite understand the whole process so the old man lathered him up and showed the child with a flat pocket comb how to shave. And then in one quick leap he's shaving for real, first just to get the feel of it, though there isn't much in the way of real hair growth, and then when he's much older, with a few days of stubble growth, having flown in from his college out of state to attend his father's funeral, shaving in the same mirror his father had. His mother's funeral comes ten years later when he's in his thirties and not married and has no children and he stares into the same mirror long and deep as if staring into a hole. He runs his hand over his balding hair and by time he reaches the back of his neck he is bald and there's been more funerals, now for friends he knew in grade school, high school, college. He's gained weight and lost it and gained it again and his face is beginning to sag a little and his eyes are set deeper and surrounded by pale wrinkles that deepen into fine lines and spread like vines along his nose and mouth until there is a mapping of time among his features. His five o' clock shadow comes in gray, then white. His teeth yellow, then they fall out and so there is dentures. Anniversaries at work tick off the clock: 10, 15, 20, 25… all gone by in a blink and a blip, with hospital visits and new prescriptions and surgeries and glasses he finds have thicker lenses every day and then are bi and then trifocal and he's staring in the mirror longer, searching for something that was lost until finally he realizes that he's not just watching himself in a mirror but watching himself watch himself with everything layered in glass like the metaphor of time split into panes, day after day, for an entire lifetime that is unreachable except in reflection; then in a blink he's young again, stepping into the bathroom, his father swooping him up, his body as light as the air in the room and his feet are nowhere solid and his eyes are shut, just for a second, and in the mirror there is no reflection because first there would need to be something there to reflect.

Silent Empire

In 1930 I was cast in a film called *Scarface* starring Paul Muni and Ann Dvorek. Howard Hughes produced. He had been a childhood friend of mine, Howard had; meaning we grew up together in Houston. Our fathers were actually in business together and collaborated on the two-cone roller bit, which could be used by oil prospectors of the day to drill in places usually unreachable by humans, which is something you may or may not know about. They made a fortune leasing their invention instead of selling them through Howard Sr.'s Hughes Tool Company.

Our families grew up on the same block of the well to do back in those days: a straight cut through the wealthiest part of the Houston suburbs, a well paved road with wrought iron fences lining every yard and gates that all had their owners' initials welded in large gold letters to the bars which stood between two brick colonnades with white steeples at their tops.

I guess you could say me and Howard were best friends.

When we were young we built two-way radios from the pieces of an electrical doorbell so we could communicate at night from our bedrooms. Howard was always the brains of the operation. He came up with some clever little gadgets and was always looking up to the sky and thinking deeply and saying things I rarely understood. I wasn't smart in the way he was. I preferred pretend. I was an actor and I guess in a sense you could say I had the looks out of the two of us. But this was quite a long time ago. Eons in fact. Howard has been dead since 1970 and I'm on my way out the door as well.

I had my 89th birthday just a week ago. After my children and their children and even some of their children left the festivities I found an unmarked package on the front porch of my home. The package contained a weathered manila envelope which had the date 1951 written in fading pen ink. I scanned the year in my mind and came up blank. Things had happened sure, but nothing I could foresee being important enough for there to be an unmarked envelope sent to me some forty odd years later.

Without thinking much more about it I opened the envelope and inside was a key along with a letter from Howard that read:

> Dear Robert,
>
> I'm writing you this in advance and only under the strictest confidence that you will in fact receive this package at the appointed time, whereby I'm sure I will

*have passed, and if all goes accordingly you yourself will
not be far from the grave. That is why I have waited, or
more importantly why I am waiting to have this delivered
until a date I have seen fit. What lies beyond the door
this key will open is by far one of the most important
discoveries I believe the United States could ever hope
to have. And now that being said I cannot disclose too
much in this letter, nor can I say that I'm very proud of
my involvement in what's to come out of that door, but it
was a prospect I couldn't pass up and I thought of it as
vitally important, no matter how devilish the ends, you
know me old friend, it's never the ends that concerned me,
only the chase, and the rarefied moments of glory that
proceeded from the acceleration of my own life's drive. I
never looked back and I never gave in. Remember, I always
made it out ahead and now that it's all said and done
damned be damned.*

You're Friend,

Howard Hughes

I read the letter and inspected the key for several
moments. It was no secret that by the end of his life
Howard was totally withdrawn from the world. He'd
been on a path of destruction for as long as I knew him:
he'd killed a man with one of his many cars while living in
Hollywood and possibly paid people off to be acquitted
of the charges, on several occasions he was known to pull
a fork from his breast pocket which he used to inspect
the size of his vegetables. He had men paid to follow
women he found interesting. He was nearly incinerated

in two plane crashes. Once, for no apparent reason, he spent four months locked in a room watching reel after reel of film, subsisting on candy bars and milk, not even leaving to bathe or use the facilities, instead urinating and defecating in discarded bottles.

I wasn't around for much of this but I've heard from a few of his aids that upon his readmission to the world Howard looked more like a Nosferatu wax sculpture, with his nails wildly long and nearly black with filth and his hair dark with detritus and grease. His face: slick with a patina of dirt and dried sweat, had sunken in from the malnutrition and weight loss over the period, and his clothes were tattered, stained, and stunk worse than the city's sewer system.

To say that Howard Hughes was a man of mystery is an understatement and to say he was a genius may give more clout than is necessary to a man with the sheer will of his mind to at once influence the world and at the same time remain isolated and sinister in his nihilistic obsessions.

He very well could have been evil.

Back to the start: When we were still in our teens Howard started taking flight lessons. He was fourteen I believe, and shortly thereafter he moved to California to audit some classes at Caltech or some such school. I believe he was more interested in aviation than he was any other pursuit, and during this period it showed in the frenetic letters he sent to me from the various hotels and apartments he stayed in while on the coast. I wrote back with admiration and showed interest in joining him. He had known that I wanted to act in pictures and after one of these letters he wrote back telling me to come along and start on my dreams. He was just starting to get into the Hollywood scene, the so-called Golden Age of Hollywood, and I was thrilled to be along for the ride.

I first arrived in California in the late 20s, star stuck and tired from the train ride. My father had afforded me a hefty allowance and told me that he wanted me to make something of myself out there. He said that I was to be my own man, despite his own allegiance to Howard Sr., and that he was proud I was leaving his trades and paving my own way.

The first few months were dull. Howard had set up some auditions for me but I never got a word back on anything. When I did it was for the B-pictures being produced by the Big Five for deferments and contractual obligations. These films were lower than average "B" movies and were rarely seen by the public, instead being stored in warehouses where auditors could count them and make tallies on clipboards. It was all a fraud.

Howard knew I could have used his name and gotten any part I liked but aside from his setting things up I wanted to do it on my own, just as my father had wished, I too hoped to become my own man, living apart from the Hughes name.

When I said I was 'cast' in the film Scarface what I really meant was I made an appearance in the film, a cameo if you will. It's a very short shot and it takes some investigation to really even get a glimpse of me but I'm there. If you've ever seen the movie I'm sure you'll recall the ending, (which you may or may not know stirred up a lot of controversy) when Tony (Paul Muni) and 'Cesca'

(Ann Dvorak) are held up in Tony's apartment and are surrounded by police. At one point Tony's attempting to seal the windows and a stray bullet hits Cesca and she slowly (and quite dramatically, to the point of being humorous) dies on a couch. Shortly thereafter the film cuts to the street level where the chief of police is yelling orders to an officer who's outside of the frame. If you look in the background you'll see three officers in a kind of semi-circle. I'm first from the left. After only a second or two I do a pivot move and kneel behind a parked motorcycle, disappearing entirely.

After that it was all roles that involved me wearing heavy masks or full body suits and latex make-up and uncomfortable straps and was just an all-around humiliating time for me personally.

During this time Howard was beginning to focus more on his real passion–aviation–and in the 1930s I lost him for a while. I ended up moving back to Texas while he moved all around, sending only sporadic and brief letters that to me seemed a bit esoteric as he was unable to "disclose" what he was working on. It was "classified" and was deemed "underground operations" by all the parties involved.

I found out later these parties were some of the top U.S. Intelligence Agencies and Military Enterprises, although at the time I questioned whether Howard was starting to really crack up, beyond the obsessive-compulsive disorder and the slew of other various mental illnesses I imagine he suffered. I know after the crashes he became addicted to Codeine, and was said to have injected it in front of aids or other workers and business partners, showing no reservations when shooting up in front of any public attendants at whatever restaurant or shop he happened to be at when stricken by the pain that pervaded him the rest of his life.

In Houston I'd started to oversee some business ventures my father had gotten himself into without much thought of the end result and if acting was what I was good at then acting was what I did—in meetings and various day to day operations consisting of contract signage and payments made to various people. The whole thing was dizzying, but I remained composed. In return my father paid me abundantly for my talents. I made more from these dealings than I would have had I stayed in California and continued trying to further my already dead career.

After the war I regained communication with Howard, in early '46-47. Out of the blue I received a letter from him stating he'd be back in Texas for a brief stint and we met several times, catching up on what he could talk about and me telling him of my dealings with my father.

He looked sickly in those days. He wore a mustache to cover a scar he'd gotten in one of his crashes, which made him look older. He told me all about flying and breaking speed records and how it felt to almost die, which he didn't seem to put much thought into. I noticed he seemed even more distant than he had when he'd first started getting into pictures and even when we were young. There was an aura of darkness around him which led me to believe he'd been carrying secrets around with him for a very long while that were toxic to his body and mind. His face was nearly blue with discolor; I could see the veins under his eyes and in his hands. He was forty one years old at that point but looked like a corpse of a hundred. It was not pleasant. I often made excuses to leave our meetings early out of the actual fear I felt looking at him for too long.

By 1950 I entirely lost contact with him. I was still living in Houston. I was married and raising children. My father had set me up to front one of his bigger businesses; an energy provider called Franklin Electric, which in the early forties and on into the 1980s was one of the largest energy providers in Texas, you may know.

The key Howard put in the envelope opened a lock box here in Houston. He must have had one of his many employees come here and deliver these things, setting up the lock box and preparing the envelope for the date of its delivery.

Inside were several sheathes of paper, government documents revealing the many projects Howard was involved in during the war. The bulk of the papers revolve around an unnamed project Howard had worked on. Howard wrote in his notes:

> When the project was first founded I was the first to be contacted because of my engineering background and standings with the media, public, etc. I was called into an office in Washington D.C., whereby I was told of the intentions and prerogatives of several men in suits and dry faces. They needed a representative. The presidents that had come out of the previous eras had been enough to sate the country, but as they said, 'Today we usher in a new era, one not founded on basic beliefs and principles,

and we need a new kind of representative for these new times.' I agreed with them whole heartedly and within a few days I was holed up in a bunker working with several men and women divided into teams which were in charge of creating this fully automated device.

They knew with the dropping of the atomic bomb that they'd need a representative, one with an almost indomitable will and never feigning public image— someone, or something, that could thus articulate and make clear their message. They wanted to be heard. It would need to be automated, artificial, they told me. It was the most complex job I'd ever worked on, more so even than an aircraft, which paled in comparison to this design.

It would need to represent an entire nation; it would have to stand before the entire world. They were forced to traipse back into the murky depths of History to conjure up pasts they only knew from their own white lies. Endless files and source material and DNA analysis and testimony from relative's decades removed, centuries even. All in an attempt to concoct the Perfect Pitch; this grouping of components exacting in its endless repetition of choreographed symphonies and sonnets and monologues.

Particularly at that moment there was the rather large and for some, a seemingly endless labyrinth of questions surrounding the atomic bomb that was to be dropped upon the world at their bidding. But that was later. For them there were more pressing concerns, and after months of planning and research and development on the part of several High Order Individuals, The project was put into full effect and given carte blanche with the understanding that there'd be a ready prototype in five months.

Originally there were 20 members of the development team, all younger people, mostly male, with bald heads who wore their white lab coats scrubbed clean and placed fresh in lockers by hygienists whose sole job was to keep the entire facility sparkling each night. (Also two advisers not counted here.)

With the looming deadline and a lot of work to be done they brought on extra personnel who made the total number 36 (four of whom would later be taken off the project for thinking they were smarter than everyone else.) This made the total number of team members involved (again this doesn't include advisers) 28, who worked in two divisions set up like a hierarchy....

Like all systems, human or non-, the device was not perfect, and the men running it were even further from perfection. I'd been dismissed shortly after device was finished and the schematics I devised and all the notes I took were confiscated from me, stolen really, but men in my position are not ones to have things taken without having a plan for taking them back and now I leave them to you, should you still be alive by time all this information reached you....

What was he trying to tell me? Or am I simply looking too far into this? I poured over the notes and had no idea.

He'd worked on a highly secretive project for the government creating a device that was meant to influence people, nations. But that could be anything. And was my observation about teeth an even valid point? What was he trying to tell me and what did he expect me to do? I just didn't know.

I've been retired for 24 years now. My mother and father have been dead some time. After my father's death a lot of his assets were deferred to me but it turned out that where once there had been a fortune there was now debt. He was no business mogul. Not like Howard, although I'm sure if Howard's legacy were brought to its full light there'd be more holes than there are stars in the sky. The difference between the two men was that my father, as driven as he was, didn't know much about the world he entered with Howard Sr. He was more along for the ride, and when he branched out on his own he very much was successful in a few fields, the energy business for instance, but with all the other investments and small pop deals and bought up businesses he just couldn't make it all work. By the end all that was left were the energy company, which I ran until 1970, whereby it was bought out by one of our top competitors and eventually shut down; and a restaurant chain, which he sold in the years just before his death. This is how I feel about myself and Howard. He has a legacy. I have nothing but a small savings which I've kept for a rainy day. I'm all by myself now. My kids are all gone and making their way through their own lives with kids of their own. I get calls sometimes, but it's never for anything important. I think they just check up on me to make sure I'm still alive.

My wife passed in 1990, she was ten years younger than I am, stubborn as a bull. She kept on right until the end, when she was struck by a dairy truck. Morbidly ironic way for her to go to: she had been lactose intolerant her entire life.

I guess everyone thinks I've gone a little off the deep end since she was killed, that I'm getting 'senile' or have one of the many brain deteriorating disorders so common in people my age. I loved Welma, sure. She was my life and I was faithful to her but the way I was raised, the way I just happened to come up and see the world didn't really allow me to express certain things, and now that she's gone I guess I'm more lonely than anything. I just want someone to be here, to talk to, and to sit with. If Howard were still alive and read these words he'd call me a coward, but I can't help being scared sometimes.

About a year ago I went to my primary doctor. His name is Sanjar. My daughter Karen took me on her day off of work and I told her that it was just a check-up but it wasn't. I was really going because I'd been getting light-headed, not just the occasional little buzz and the wobbly knees but whole days of dizziness and fatigue and feeling like I was falling down a well inside. It was awful. So I went to Sanjar and had him hook me up to his machines and find out what was what.

He told me that the scans showed nothing and that he'd have to run more tests. A series of these damned tests in which he'd draw blood and poke and prod me with God knows what then run me through more machines and make me drink different colored liquids and scan my brain and do all types of madness. I said no thanks. He insisted I get the tests done if it was as bad as I said it was but I just said that maybe I over exaggerated a little and that I'd be ok.

In the car Karen sensed something wasn't right and she asked me how it went, not out of concern but as an interrogative type of test in which she already knew the answer. I told her it went fine. "Just a check-up," I said to her.

"Dad. Come on. What's going on?" she asked, glancing over at me with a serious look on her face.

"He wanted to run some tests. I've been getting light headed; dizzy spells. I told him no."

"Why did you do that?" She said.

"Because I don't want to be a pin cushion and test subject and feel humiliated because I get dizzy." I said.

She went on and I went on. I had to explain that I wasn't getting any younger and that at my age all the things that other people worry about are everyday things with me and others my age: Heart disease, stroke, cancer, sleep deprivation, memory loss, and weight gain, all of it. Death is closer to you than it's ever been, every day I said. "...And so I don't feel like spending what could be my last day on earth cooped up in the hospital with needles all in me and the lights and the gowns. It's a theater. It's a circus and I won't be a part of it."

She sighed and said nothing else the whole ride home.

It's taken me longer than I thought to get through the papers as they were inherited from Howard, it doesn't help that my head spins, and when I stand I have to brace myself against whatever stands close enough to keep myself from falling over. Every time I think I'm nearing the end, more seem to appear. His digressions are endless, the web of the project seems to extend far and wide into seemingly every other conspiracy in the History of The United States of America, but there's still no answer as to what the project was.

I'm starting to think it's all an elaborate fiction he created to give me something to do, to work out. In his diseased mind maybe he always saw me as this bored man with nothing much happening in life. Howard did that sometimes. Put these judgments on people and then did what he could to quote unquote "help" them. What am I to do with what I've been given? There's no way for me to do anything but read and to wonder, maybe he was making this up as some sort of "treatment" for a movie script idea, then, when it went unfinished or he just stopped caring he's now, even in his grave, trying to pass it off to me as real just for his own amusement.

I came across this passage yesterday: *It was as if I were directing a film, as if I'd stumbled onto the soundstage of Fritz Lang's Metropolis, everyone in white and ordered and doing their part while somewhere else in the world another group of individuals was doing theirs. Ordered Chaos; that is the structure. Like the ripples of a large stone thrown into the ocean.*

In the late fifties I considered penning a memoir about my years in Hollywood with Howard. I don't know why I'm thinking of this but I am. It was a very bad idea from the start but in retrospect I think I was trying to hold onto that old life; that youth that always felt wasted but is so sweet when gazed back upon: The freedom of it, the energy. That's what I wanted to capture, and so I resigned my duties at Franklin Electric for a year to the Plant's Second Superior, Ronald Coburn, and set about fleshing out what I thought would not only be an interesting and heartfelt book, but for me would be a journey back into the past.

I was going to call it "Best of Friends: My Life with Howard Hughes" or something along those lines. Welma was very supportive; her only insistence was that I finish the book by the time our fourth child was born that April.

Maybe that had put pressure on me, or maybe I was just naïve thinking I could write a book with no formal teaching and very little interest in the craft. Of course, I never finished it. I decided to abandon it after the stack of pages grew to over a thousand random notes and false starts, most of them about Howard and his antics, none adding up to an endearing piece of autobiographical literature, that's for sure. The whole mess of it went into the trash. Welma watched mournfully and gave her condolences. A few weeks later our son, Kohl, was born, bringing a new beacon of hope into my otherwise futile attempts at living a productive life.

If there's one thing I've learned about getting old it's that no matter how hard you fight it, no matter how fast and hard you try to paddle upstream, the waves of time will always wash you back and there's nothing left to do at that point but float along. You're just so weak and tired and sick of trying.

And that's how I feel now and I float, just as I did when I moved back to Houston and took the job at my father's plant. It wasn't necessarily what I wanted out of life or something I enjoyed doing, obviously there were other things, and I'd tried my hardest to make them work but that's another thing about this life: It doesn't always work out how you have it planned. Now the current's faster and I'm swept along, it's harder to turn and look back through the haze coming off the surface of the water, or in the swirls as I'm taken under, caught in the undertow, not knowing which way is up or if I really care to.

I put Howard's papers in a new envelope with a new date. 1999. Give myself five years. If I'm not gone by then maybe I'll take them back out and see if I can even still read them. If not I'm enclosing a short note to whoever finds them:

> *To Whom It May Concern,*
>
> *If you find these papers and are interested in their contents do what you will with them. I'm afraid that although they were originally intended for me I just didn't know how to handle it. Maybe you will.*
>
> *Robert Franklin, 1994*

I left the note along with the papers in a trunk of my belongings that I guess was kind of like a Time Capsule I'd left up in my room and hadn't been in in years. There are all types of things in there: old stills of films I'd been in, my dozen or so headshots sent out to agents and agencies in hopes I'd land a big deal, the radio (mine at least) that Howard and I had constructed as children, yellowed scripts, and various other memorabilia, unimportant to everyone except for me, opening it brought a rush of memories that actually made the hairs on my neck tingle and my skin goose bump; head felt light as a carnival balloon.

The last thing I picked up was the Scarface poster I'd taken from the theater after the premiere.

It's a crude colored pencil drawing of two men in a tussle; one of the men has his hand over the other's face so his features are obscured. Howard's name appears very large and prominent and then there's a short list of the stars. In the bottom right hand corner is a woman in a red dress with what appears to be smoke billowing out of her stomach.

I'd tagged along with Howard and am probably in a few of the pictures taken from that evening but even now I'm lost in the shadow, everyone more focused on the man Howard Hughes, even myself here now all these years later thinking about him and how no one knows my name, and no one cares to ask, "Who's that guy?" just as I'm sure no one cares to search for me in the end of the film that I guess could be called the culmination of my entire film career, which is a sad thing indeed.

For Howard it was just another venture, a tiny insignificant thing that in the end would mean very little and most likely be only half-remembered in the light of all the other things he went on to do, but for me it was a

very big deal. As I said it was a culmination, the catharsis. That role for me was more than a role; it came to
embody something, or encased it, like a cocoon encas-
ing a caterpillar which will one day become, through its
metamorphosis, a butterfly. It changed me, from the man
I had been to someone who could have ended up meaning something. It was that conviction that kept me going
for a little while after the shoot had ended and the film
was done.

I remember the day as if it were yesterday: It was a
damn hot day in California. The street the set was on was
like a funnel for the rays of sunlight that just absolutely
hammered us. I had sweat stains on the uniform they had
me wear which was wool, making the whole ordeal that
much worse, and we were outside for most of the time,
shooting and reshooting this one scene, the last scene. I
didn't really have to be there I guess. I was only in the
film for a minute or two but I liked the atmosphere of
sets like that, the really big pictures: so much action, so
much energy hovering in the air. It's really intoxicating if
you've experienced it; invigorating, as if you were in the
presence of God or something so large it even paled the
deity's own features and made the world itself the object
of holy perfection and grace.

When it came time for the last few shots I readied
myself and went through my ritual, which involved some
heavy breathing and a quick exercise like routine; mostly
jumping up and down in quick steady bursts and clap-
ping my hands.

Howard had come to the set that day. I don't know if
it was specifically to see me or if he was there on business
but I'll never forget it. He walked up to me. The director

had already called action so it was right in the middle of the shoot. He noticed something, Howard did, and he wanted to correct it, wanted to correct me on how I was holding the gun. I had obviously only seen how other actors held their sidearm in detective pictures and noir films. I had no experience with guns, had never even held something close to one before that day. Howard took the thing from me and said, "Don't hold it like that, it makes you look weak. If you're going to do it, do it right," And he showed me how he felt I should be holding it, gripping it tightly and raising it up with his arm perfectly straight, one eye closed, the other eye steady through the sight as he pulled the trigger, even though it was a prop and nothing would happen.

Mark Anthony Cronin is a lifelong Cleve-
lander. He's worked mostly in retail for
his 27 years. He currently runs Small
Victories Press with his friend John B.
Henry. This is his first book.

smallvictoriespress.com

https://www.facebook.com/mark.cronin.3152